A FATAL BITE

THEASTARR VALERIE

A Nhyira Files Mystery Book 2

A Fatal Bite

Nhyira Files Mystery Book 2

ISBN: 9781733829335

This is a work of fiction. Names, characters, places, and incidents are either a product of the author's imagination or used fictitiously. Any resemblance to actual persons, living or dead, events, or places is entirely coincidental.

Editors: Theastarr Valerie – Empress Royále Publishing
Email: empressroyalepublishing@gmail.com

Cover Design: Empress Royále Publishing

Cover Photo: "Pancakes" from StockSnap (Pixabay.com)
"Ferris Wheel" from Postermywall.com
"Magnifying Glass" from *Bru-nO* (Pixabay.com)

Empress Royále Publishing

"Everything tells a story; let us help you tell your story to the world."

Email: empressroyalepublishing@gmail.com

DEDICATION

To all the men and women who have devoted their lives to solving mysteries.

To all the Parents, Educators, Members of the Judiciary System, Medical Professionals, Mystery Lovers, Problem Solvers, Researchers, Authors…

This book is for you.

Thank you for all your hard work.

Proverbs 25:2 (KJV)

"It is the glory of God to conceal a thing: but the honour of kings is to search out a matter."

To God, the greatest mystery writer from eternity to eternity, thank You.

Chapter

B*estselling* novelist, Nhyira Enosis places her *Chocolate Macadamia Cloud Torte* in the oven. *Njapa's* 28th Annual Chocolate Festival was quickly approaching and she wanted to tweak the recipe of her famous dessert.

Two years ago she moved to *Njapa,* Celgagoas from *Grape Fjord*, Mt. Thafivin. And in that time she went from an average woman to a crime solving bestselling author. Her book - ***Veisiejai House Murder*** - was based on the real life murder case of her great-uncle, his accused wife (who spent 40 years in prison for the crime), and his ex-business partner, Rémire Embleton, aka the **real murderer**.

These days there were no murders to solve and Nhyira's heart was content.

Her great-aunt, Poet, enters the kitchen. "Sweetie, what smells so good?"

"Adding new ingredients to my torte." Nhyira sprinkles *Thalak Seeds* into the bowl.

"Ever since I returned to this house, my caloric intake has skyrocketed."

"You look good though."

"Thanks to our daily exercise regime. I'm fit as a stick," Poet notes, standing akimbo.

Nhyira puts on the oven timer. "I want this to be perfect for the festival. Mayleigh told me that a food critic will be coming into town. But shhhh, it's a secret. This is the biggest festival to date."

"Everyone wants to meet you," Poet beams.

"Nah. I think it's those pancakes of Mayleigh's that has put the town on the map. I told her she'd be famous for it one day."

"Have you seen Akio lately?"

Nhyira's countenance changes at the mention of his name. "Not really. We dated a few times, but he has been distant as of recent. For a man who said he likes me, he has a bad way of showing it."

"Maybe he found someone else," Poet counters.

"It doesn't matter," Nhyira shrugs. "I'm not interested in dating."

"You've been saying that for two years. Don't you think it's time you consider it?"

"I don't see the point."

"I want you to be happy."

"I am."

"Akio's a good man for you."

"I don't need that headache in my life," Nhyira counters, walking to the sink to wash her hands.

Akio Qvareli found himself caught between a rock and a hard place. After months of attending Bible Study at Mayleigh's house whenever he was in *Njapa*, he made the decision to accept Jesus as his personal Lord and Savior. He demonstrated this by water baptism at his church in *Kanomatton*. That was one week ago.

The topic of the month for Bible Study was on being **unequally yoked**. Although Akio liked Nhyira since the moment he saw her sitting at the diner's counter, being with her didn't feel right. Not unless she gave her life to Jesus.

As a new convert he was eager to do the right thing. So he'd made up in his mind to keep his distance when it came to her. His feelings for her couldn't be denied, but he drew the line at **disobedience**.

"The usual?" Mayleigh greets, when Akio sits at the counter.

Akio nods.

"A half dozen pancakes Chef Boada," she yells out to her executive chef.

"Coming right up," the chef responds.

For her 18th birthday, Mayleigh's father gave her the diner. And Abacus Boada had been the executive chef ever since. Through thick and thin he'd stood by her side. When her husband died, Abacus was a source of comfort. Many people thought they'd end up together, but she didn't view him that way and he showed no interest in her besides work. She enjoyed their friendship.

Abacus knocks on the kitchen window. "Pancakes are ready."

Taking the pancakes from the counter, Mayleigh hands it to Akio. "Looking for anyone in particular?"

Akio's face turns blank.

"Your eyes have been staring at the door ever since you sat down."

"This is hard, Mayleigh. I really like Nhyira, but she's made it clear that dating isn't on her mind. To top it off she's not a believer, so we can't be together," Akio sighs.

"Take it one day at a time," Mayleigh advises.

"You ready for the food critic?"

"I can't think about that right now. I'm just thankful people are coming to *Njapa*; thankful that our stigma has been completely lifted."

"I look forward to the festival food."

She laughs at Akio. "You need a wife. Even though I'm not complaining, the amount of money that you spend on food could be used to run a home."

"Hopefully one day I'll find her," Akio exhales.

"You need to get your mind off Nhyira, first," Mayleigh adds.

Akio eats his pancakes in silence. Nhyira had his heart, but he needed to give his heart fully over to Jesus. No woman was worth his soul.

Chapter

The next morning, Nhyira observes her aunt dressed to go out; a frequent occurrence that still baffled her. "Where are you off to aunty?"

Poet puts on her bracelet. "I'm going over to Lively's."

"I still can't believe that you and Ms. Higüey are friends, after all the drama that happened between you."

"We were young and made mistakes, but it's not necessary to hold grudges. We have a lot in common; may even take a trip together."

"This is the same woman who hated you for decades because she thought you ruined her relationship with the first mayor."

"Life huh? Just two years ago I was sitting in a prison cell. Yet here I am, a free woman," Poet replies.

Nhyira stares in the direction of Ms. Higüey's house. "I'm glad to see her getting out of the house. Now if only she'd respect me."

"Give her time."

"What are you two doing today?"

"**Paint and Sip** at the library."

"That sounds fun. Enjoy."

"Bye sweetie," her aunt waves, closing the door.

Nhyira heads to her backyard garden. Outside she swats a bee buzzing by her ear. Bending to pick flowers, she hears the doorbell ringing.

I'm not expecting anyone.

She heads to the front of her house and opens the door.

"Good afternoon stranger," a man greets.

"Jörn? Jörn Oberhaus?"

"If it isn't *Grape Fjord*'s Unscrambler turned crime solver turned Bestselling Author."

"That's a mouthful."

"I deserve a hug." He leans in to hug her. "You look beautiful by the way. I've been trying to get off of work for the longest time. Gran's spoken so much about you for a long time. I always believed in timing."

"Timing is everything. What brings you to Celgagoas? *Njapa* to be exact?"

"You of course."

Nhyira's eyes widen. "Me?"

"You and your town's famous chocolate festival."

"Now that sounds like a plausible response," Nhyira giggles.

"You don't believe I came here to see you?"

"How is nursing?" she asks, changing the subject.

"It's wonderful. I love working at the clinic."

"You're the only male nurse I know."

"Times are changing," he replies.

"Indeed. I was just about to head to the diner for lunch."

"Diner?" Jörn asks, still scanning her face.

"**Mayleigh's Diner**. Didn't you pass it on your way over here?"

"I only had one thing on my mind."

"Oh stop," Nhyira chuckles.

"I didn't say it was you."

"Right. Where are you staying?"

"*Holbrook Villas*."

"Oh yes, I know it," Nhyira says. "Popular hotel."

"They're known for quality."

"How long will you be staying?"

"Until after the festival."

"That's a long vacation."

"Long overdue," he replies. "I've been working hard and I wanted to vacation somewhere with potential."

Nhyira stares at him. "I don't understand. What potential?"

"When the time is right I'll share," he winks. "In the meantime, point me to the diner."

Chapter

"**It's** packed in there," Jörn observes through the window.

Nhyira smiles at him. "A lot of folks are coming in early for the festival. Hotels get booked up real fast."

"How many people come to the festival?"

"The first year I moved here, had roughly 1,000 visitors. I believe it doubled last year. The buzz this year has been huge."

"Are we going inside?"

"Yeah, but I should warn you, you may get questioned."

"I'm not afraid of questions, Nhyira. Come on," he takes her hand and escorts her inside.

Mayleigh looks up from wiping the counter and pauses. She hoped that Akio didn't come into the diner today. Seeing Nhyira with another man would never go down well.

"Hi Mayleigh," Nhyira greets.

"Who's your friend?"

"My name's Nurse Oberhaus, but friends call me Jörn."

Mayleigh shakes his hand, "Nice to meet you, Jörn. First time in our little town?"

"Yes," he nods. "This pretty lady brought me here."

"She did, did she? How do you two know each other?" Mayleigh stares austerely at Nhyira.

"Jörn and I have been mates since daycare days," Nhyira informs.

"I see," Mayleigh acknowledges. "So you know one another quite well."

"We do," Jörn beams.

Mayleigh hands him a menu. "Order anything you like, on the house."

"That's okay, I have money," Jörn hits his wallet.

Nhyira motions for him not to refuse her offer.

"I'm sorry, did I say something wrong?"

"When Mayleigh offers you a meal, you take it, no questions asked," Nhyira schools him.

"Really? I'll keep that in mind." He glances at the menu, "Any suggestions?"

"You **have** to try the *Plumberry Pancakes*."

"Plumberry?"

"They're out of this world," Nhyira continues.

"I guess I'll be having pancakes," Jörn nods, handing Mayleigh the menu.

"I'll be right back with your pancakes," Mayleigh states, walking into the kitchen.

Jörn turns his gaze to Nhyira. "Your friend seems nice. What do you do around here for fun? Seems awful quiet in this town."

"We hang out at the diner or go to the beach."

Jörn fake yawns, "Sounds boring."

"To a city boy like you."

"Don't forget you're from the big city too."

"I love it in *Njapa*. The quietness grows on you."

"I'll be the judge of that."

Nhyira squirms nervously in her seat. She hadn't expected anyone to insult the town she grew to love. It was like her second home.

The door opens and a man enters the diner.

“Nhyira?”

“Akio?”

The awkwardness between them was obvious. He rolls his eyes at Jörn.

“Oh, where are my manners?” Nhyira chuckles. “Akio Qvareli this is Jörn Oberhaus, my childhood friend and classmate. Jörn this is Akio, one of the residents.”

“Pleased to meet you,” Jörn offers his hand.

Akio shakes it hesitantly. “You too man.” He turns back to Nhyira. “How have you been?”

“Great. Trying to work on my second book.”

“It’s so weird that I haven’t seen you all these months,” Akio replies, ignoring Jörn’s presence.

“You’re a busy man. What have you been up to?”

“I live in *Kanomatton* full-time now.”

“I see. Okay cool,” Nhyira smiles weakly, trying not to look at Akio.

“Nhyira, our pancakes are here,” Jörn interjects.

“What?”

“The pancakes. Let’s eat.”

"See you around, Akio," she waves.

"Later," Akio answers. "Jörn."

"That was painful to watch," Mayleigh says when Akio sits by the counter. She hands him a plate of pancakes.

"Is that her boyfriend?"

"Not according to her."

"He likes her, I can tell," Akio speaks through clenched teeth.

"She's a good girl, why shouldn't he?"

"I've suddenly lost my appetite."

"Boy you better sit down and eat those pancakes."

"And watch Nhyira with another man?" Akio scoffs. "No thank you."

"You'll be fine."

"I can't do this, Mayleigh. Can you box it up for me?"

"Suit yourself. Abacus, hand me a box please."

Moments later Akio sits in his jeep watching Nhyira through the window.

Is she serious?

He exhales and drives off.

Chapter

4

"***Y**ou've* been spending a lot of time with Jörn," Poet notes at breakfast, a few days later. "Do you like him?"

"I don't know, maybe," Nhyira shrugs.

"Think you're ready to date now?"

"No."

"Well the way you're hanging out with that boy is considered dating or getting to know someone."

"Jörn and I go way back. I enjoy his company."

"That's how your uncle and I started," Poet adds. "The more you spend time with someone, you begin to like them."

"We're just childhood pals."

"The best relationships start off as friendships. It's an excellent foundation to have."

Nhyira puts a spoonful of cereal into her mouth. "I guess."

"What about Akio?" Poet inquires, pouring a glass of juice.

"What about him? He's obviously not interested. He even moved out of town without so much as a warning. Today was the first time I saw him since the year began."

"You two have something. I know it."

"That was the past. He's different now. I don't know how to explain it. He's still Akio, but his behavior has changed."

"Bad change?"

"No, but—"

"You'll figure it out," Poet states, sipping her drink.

"Figure what out?"

"Your feelings for these men," Poet replies.

"This is what I was trying to avoid; feelings and stuff."

"You're not a 22 year old anymore. Soon you'll be 25."

"I still have a few months."

"Time's flying. We're almost in 2001."

"Slow down aunty."

"I am. Anyway, I made you *Quayap Soup* for lunch."

"Yummy. I love your soup. Maybe I can share some with Jörn. We're heading to the beach."

"That's the fifth time this week." Poet pours soup in two containers and hands them to Nhyira.

"He's not accustomed to beaches. There's none in *Grape Fjord*."

"You two have fun."

"We will," Nhyira chimes, grabbing the containers.

"I love when we visit the beach. I've enjoyed spending time with you. I wish it didn't have to end," Jörn declares.

"It's good being in the company of a familiar face."

"Is that all I am to you?"

"We're friends."

"I've liked you ever since I can remember," he reveals.

"I'm not ready to date," Nhyira retorts.

"I'm not asking you to date. I'm asking that you consider marrying me."

Nhyira begins to gag on her soup. "Say what?"

"I want us to start a relationship that'll lead to marriage."

"Marriage you say? I don't know about that."

"What's the problem? We both know each other. We know what we want. Why not marriage?"

"I'm enjoying this stage in my life and marriage is not on my mind. I mean it pops in my head from time to time, but definitely not something I'm considering," Nhyira says.

"Think about it."

"There's nothing to think about, Jörn."

He brushes away a strand of her hair. "Are you telling me you don't feel that?"

"All I feel is breeze."

Cupping her face, Jörn kisses her. Nhyira doesn't pull away.

"So you feel it too?" he asks, moments later.

"I-I don't know."

"We have friendship and chemistry. What we have is special."

Akio's feet shook as he sat in his car. His mind flashed back to moments prior. Jogging on the beach to spend time in prayer, he passed Nhyira and her **friend** kissing on the beach. They hadn't even noticed him. Exhaling a long breath, he resists the urge to cry. When did he become such a wimp? The woman clearly didn't want him and he had to get over her. No matter how much he tried to disregard it, there was no refuting his unfathomable feelings for her. He was in love.

Chapter

5

28th Annual Njapa Chocolate Festival

Jörn and Nhyira watched as the waves danced across the ocean. Although a few feet away from the festival's entrance, they wanted to spend this moment together before the townsfolk started questioning them. From the distance Nhyira spotted her aunt, their neighbor, and Mayleigh. However, there was no sign of Akio.

Nhyira hadn't realized she cared, but brushed off the feelings.

"You were right, Nhyira. This festival is huge. Look at all those people." He takes her hand. "I'm with the most beautiful woman in the world."

"Want me to take that?" she says, referring to the torte in his hand.

"No, I got it. Too bad they don't judge on the food, because you'd be a shoo-in for winner."

Giggling, Nhyira looks at Jörn. Things were so easy with him. Coming from the same background, they had a lot in common.

"How long are you going to hide in this tent?" Mayleigh asks Akio, at the tent's entrance. "Go out and have fun. You love the chocolate festival."

"I'm not in a celebratory mode, not while she's here with him. Look at them over there taking pictures. Are they dating?" Akio whines.

"I don't know much about their relationship, but they do spend a lot of time together. Maybe you can ask Poet."

Akio glances over at the older woman. Mustering up the courage, he exits the tent and treads toward her. "Good night Mrs. Veisiejai."

"Akio, I told you to call me Poet."

"I respect my elders."

"You appear sullen, what's the matter?"

"Why is Nhyira here with that man?"

"She's a grown woman and can make her own decisions. I think their relationship is serious. I've heard talk about marriage."

"Marriage?" Akio probes.

"As I said, she's a grown woman. But, she's stated that you two haven't been in communication lately. Why should her relationship status matter to you?"

"She said that?"

"What's going on?"

"I can't explain it; sorting out some things in my life."

Poet places her hand on his shoulder and stares at him like a son. "All I can say is if you love her, fight for her."

Nhyira cuts a slice of her torte for Jörn and brings it over to their seat.

"No thank you, I don't eat sweets," he declines.

"You're at a chocolate festival."

"I came to keep you company. Don't understand why anyone would dedicate an entire festival to chocolate."

Staring at him in annoyance, Nhyira sighs. "Sorry our town isn't as fascinating as your city. But, this festival is a part of the town's legacy. We grow our own cocoa beans and make organic chocolate. The revenue from the festival helps to fund the hospital and local schools."

"The irony," he scoffs, "since too many sweets could put one in the hospital."

"That's where you have it all wrong. Our chocolate is sweetened with *Thalak Seeds*; the healthiest sweetener on the planet. You won't get sick from our chocolate. No high sugar levels or anything."

"Well, aren't you the poster woman for *Njapa*?" he teases.

"Are you mocking me?" Nhyira snaps.

"I don't get it. But, I'm happy to learn. Tell me more about the history of this town."

"Do you really want to know?"

Jörn squeezes her hand. "I do."

Chapter

6

The townsfolk gathered at Mayleigh's diner after the festival.

"Jörn, did you enjoy our chocolate festival?" Mayleigh inquires.

He smiles at Nhyira, and then returns his gaze to Mayleigh. "Being there with Nhyira made it even better. You have a good thing going."

"Time for a nightcap to celebrate a successful festival," Mayleigh announces.

"Is that him?" Nhyira looks over at one of the patrons. "The food critic?"

"Yes, act natural," Mayleigh whispers.

"How else am I supposed to act? What are you going to serve him?"

"When Abacus finishes washing the dishes, I'm going to give him a special serving of my *Plumberry Pancakes* for starters, and then he can order whatever he wants. He came specifically for the pancakes."

"I hope he writes you an excellent review," Nhyira encourages her friend.

"Me too," Mayleigh replies, nervously.

World renowned restaurateur and food critic, Cyprian Iwai glances around, observing the guests in the quaint, but large diner. He jots down a few comments, noting the first-rate service from the owner, Mayleigh Antao.

He was the man you wanted in your corner. Not only was he a superb chef, but his restaurant reviews placed many businesses on the world map.

Mayleigh stands in the kitchen nervously mixing the batter for the pancakes. She'd asked all the staff to leave the diner early, so that the food critic could judge the pancakes from the one who invented the recipe.

Even her executive chef was ordered out. She wanted no distractions as she added the special ingredient to the batter, just for the critic.

No one knew about her special ingredient. This particular batch started off as a mistake, but if all went right with the review, more customers would flock to the diner.

"Is the diner always this full?" Jörn repeats, remembering his first visit.

"Every day," Nhyira giggles.

"No one cooks in this town?" he derides.

“I think people just enjoy each other’s company. The diner affords us a safe place to hang out.”

“Safe? Is this a dangerous community?”

“I didn’t mean it that way, Jörn.”

“Do you know what you’re ordering?”

“I haven’t decided,” Nhyira laughs, coyly.

“Do you know how cute you are? I’m glad that we’ve reconnected.”

“It’s been fun. I’m sorry you have to leave soon.”

“I can always visit or you could move back to *Grape Fjord*.”

“My life’s here in *Njapa*.”

“I hope one day you’ll change your mind.”

“There’s nothing to change, I’m happy here.”

“I didn’t say you weren’t. Food’s here.”

They begin to eat. Nhyira meticulously cuts the pancakes into small squares.

“Where’s your friend?”

“Who?”

“That man you introduced me to,” Jörn replies.

“Akio? I have no clue,” she shrugs.

“I’m surprised he’s not here. He was watching you for the entire festival.”

“I wonder why he didn’t at least say hi.”

“Does it matter?”

“No, but—”

“Someone call *75,” one of the patrons yell.

The other patrons start to scream. **“HE’S DEAD. HE’S DEAD!”**

Chapter

M*ayleigh* runs out of the kitchen. "What's wrong?"

"That man, he just started to choke on the pancakes," a woman sitting in the booth next to Mr. Iwai, cries.

"M-My pancakes?" Mayleigh stutters.

Minutes later, sirens are heard. Officers swarm the diner.

"Please step away from the victim ma'am," an officer snaps, pushing Mayleigh.

"Excuse me? This is my diner. What's going on?"

The woman's dinner companion speaks up. "He was eating the pancakes, writing notes and then all of a sudden he began to choke."

"And no one helped him?" the rude officer questions.

"I tried to do CPR," the man exhales, "but he was already dead."

"D-Dead?" Mayleigh squeals.

"Sir, can you give that officer your statement? You too miss," the officer says to the witnesses.

Nhyira stands next to her friend. "Mayleigh, what's happening?"

Holding her head shivering, Mayleigh begins to panic. "I don't know. He's dead."

"But how?"

"A witness said they saw him choking on my pancakes."

"Did he eat too fast?"

"I don't know, Nhyira. I don't know. Someone died because of my pancakes; a popular someone. This is not the publicity I need."

"Everything's going to be okay," Nhyira encourages.

The rude officer clinks a glass. "Excuse me ladies and gentlemen, sorry to cut this party short, but this is now an active crime scene. Everyone please stay where you are for questioning."

One by one the patrons nod their heads in agreement.

"First of all, who are you?" Nhyira asks.

The officer flashes his badge. "Officer Zevallos."

"Okay, that's a good start. I've never seen you around here before," Nhyira notes.

"I'm a transfer. Wait, I'm the one who should be asking questions. Who are you?"

She extends her hand to the officer. "Nhyira Enosis, local resident of *Njapa*."

"She's being modest. This woman is a bestselling crime solving author," Jörn adds.

Nhyira gives him a look.

"Okay Ms. Enosis, did you see what happened to the victim?" the officer questions.

"No, we were sitting on the other side of the diner."

"Then you serve no purpose in this investigation, unless of course you remember something," he states.

Mayleigh wipes tears from her eyes. "Am I being arrested?"

Officer Zevallos turns to Mayleigh. "Right now I have to take you in for questioning. Is there anyone you'd like to call? Husband? Children?"

"Don't have any of those," Mayleigh replies.

"You'll have to come with me then," Officer Zevallos points to the exit.

"I'm coming too," Nhyira adds.

"How can I help?" Jörn asks Nhyira.

“Can you go to the mansion and ask my aunt to send an overnight outfit and my toiletries for me? I need to be there for Mayleigh, but I don’t have time to go home for the items.”

“Sure,” Jörn answers willingly, “text me the address.”

Nhyira exits the diner with Mayleigh and the officer.

Chapter

Njapa Jailhouse

"**How's** she?" Jörn inquires, handing Nhyira a bag, thirty minutes later.

"She hasn't said anything since we arrived. I think she's still in shock."

"You think she did it?"

"Mayleigh would never hurt anyone," Nhyira cries.

"Maybe the critic was allergic to something in the pancakes," Jörn states, offering a possibility.

"Impossible. Mayleigh asked Mr. Iwai if he had any allergies, before he came to the restaurant."

"This was a pre-planned dining then?"

"Yes," Nhyira nods. "She's been raving about his arrival for weeks. So everyone knew he was coming."

"Everyone? Could it have been one of the workers?"

"By everyone I meant Mayleigh and her closest friends. No one else knew, not even her staff."

"Maybe we should question all of her friends."

Nhyira lowers her voice. "They live out of town."

"From what I've read in your book," Jörn says, "being *'out of town'* doesn't exempt you from murder."

Nhyira's mind flashes back to the details that led to the conviction of her great-uncle's killer. Mr. Embleton had been out of town, but according to her aunt, he secretly stalked her uncle. No one saw the man, so Poet spent forty years in prison for a crime she didn't commit; an error that the Celgagoan judiciary system didn't want to make again.

In the two years since Poet's release, the government made an edict to give every criminal a lawyer and fair trial. Of course criminals were few in numbers in *Njapa*.

"Nhyira Enosis?"

She looks up at Officer Zevallos. "Yes?"

"Mayleigh wants to see you."

"Is her lawyer there?"

"She asked to speak to you before the lawyer comes in."

Nhyira walks into the interrogation room. Inside she attempts to hug Mayleigh, but an officer pulls her off.

"No touching," the burly officer barks.

"What's your problem?" Nhyira quips.

"Sit Nhyira," Mayleigh whispers.

"Why are you whispering?"

"I don't want anyone to hear what we're talking about."

"I'm sure the room is rigged with listening devices."

Mayleigh motions to the officer standing near the door. "I'm referring to him."

"Why'd you ask to see me?"

"I've been framed."

"Not again," Nhyira whines. "Why am I a crime magnet?"

"You have a gift. You genuinely care for people and for true justice to prevail."

"Do you know who would want to see you behind bars? Any enemies?"

"No and no."

"Could someone have tampered with the batter?"

Mayleigh shakes her head. “Not possible. I made it from scratch. I hadn’t opened any of the ingredients. They were purchased especially for that batter.”

“What do you want me to do in the meantime?” Nhyira continues, noting her friend’s apprehension.

“I need you to go back to the restaurant and search for clues.”

“I don’t have keys and that place is an active crime scene. I don’t think the officers will allow me in there.”

“Akio has spare keys.”

“A-Akio?” Nhyira stutters.

“I gave him the keys earlier this week when he came for Bible Study. I left the diner early and asked him to close up for me. I told him to hold on to it for future meetings.”

“Bible study you say? You’re serious about your God.”

“I pray that you find HIM for yourself one day.”

“That won’t be necessary. My life’s fine as it is. Don’t need anyone telling me how to live it.”

“Being a follower of Christ isn’t about rules and regulations. It’s about a relationship with Jesus and fulfilling the purpose for which God has created us,” Mayleigh explains.

“Again,” Nhyira yawns, “I’m not interested in any relationship with any man; human or spirit.”

“I’ll pray for you.”

"While you do that, I have to muster up the courage to ask Akio for those keys."

"I'm sure it won't be a problem. He's on his way here."

"Why didn't you tell me?"

"Didn't think it'd matter," Mayleigh shrugs. "Aren't you two friends?"

Nhyira rolls her eyes. "Not even close."

Akio strolls into the *Njapa Jailhouse* ready to help his friend in her time of need. The last person he wanted to see was Nhyira's supposed boyfriend.

What is he doing here?

Akio clears his throat. "Are you being helped?"

"Excuse me?" Jörn turns around to face him.

"What are you doing here? Are they questioning you too?"

"I'm here to support Nhyira."

At the mention of her name from his lips, Akio grits his teeth.

Get a grip man. You don't even know him. Don't let him get to you.

"I thought you worked somewhere else?" Jörn continues.

"Not that it's any of your business, but I came to see Mayleigh."

"Cool. I'm sure she needs as much support as she can get."

"Where is Nhyira?"

"Right over there, talking to an officer," Jörn points.

"What were you speaking to Akio so cozily about?" Jörn asks, slightly jealous.

Nhyira dangles keys in the air. "He gave me this."

"Keys?"

"Do you want to help me with an investigation?"

"I get to be in the **Nhyira Files**?" Jörn exclaims. "When do we start?"

"Right now. Let's go!"

Chapter

Poet hands Nhyira a cup of *Freesia Spice Latte.* "What time did you come in?"

"Hmmm thanks." Nhyira sips the drink. "I just got in. It was a long night."

"How's Mayleigh?"

"I'd say she's very calm for a woman accused of murder."

"I wish I'd done that back then. Maybe if I was able to speak up for myself, I wouldn't have spent all those decades in prison."

"Aunty, I hope one day your mind can be freed from the years of imprisonment. It's one thing to be physically free, but when you're mentally free, that's a freedom no one can truly explain."

"What are you up to today?" Poet asks, changing the subject.

"Jörn and I are going by the diner to begin an investigation."

"*Jörn and I*? Wow aren't you all chummy," Poet notes.

"What about you?"

"Lively and I are going to *Kanomatton* to site see. I lived there for forty years, but haven't been anywhere," she laughs sarcastically.

"This friendship of yours is growing."

"She's nice once you get to know her."

"That's up to her. I tried for months to no avail."

"Keep trying."

"I think I hear Jörn's horn."

"Not taking your car? That's unlike you."

"He wants to pick me up," Nhyira shrugs.

"Gentlemanly. I'm glad that you're getting comfortable enough for a man to exercise his chivalrous duty."

"You're so 1950s, aunty."

"Watch it, lil girl."

They both laugh.

"I hope you find a beau in *Kanomatton*."

"My days for that are over. No one can compare to my Kavos. I don't want to start over with a new man."

"You never know what life will throw your way. Love is unpredictable."

"Are you in love with Jörn?"

"I'm making a general statement. I'm not in love with anyone."

"We'll talk about this later. Your gentleman's calling."

Jörn opens the passenger door for Nhyira.

"Thank you kind sir," Nhyira grins, mimicking a foreign accent.

"I love what you did with your hair."

"You noticed?" she playfully strokes it.

"I notice everything about you. Like how your eyes squint when you're deep in thought. Or how excited you get when your favorite song plays on the radio. I notice everything."

"I guess I chose the right investigative partner."

"I want to be more than that to you," he comments, pulling out of the driveway.

"We've spoken about this already."

"Not in detail."

"Can we focus on today's investigation?"

“How come we’re here so early?” Jörn asks.

“We had to arrive before the officers.”

“Is this illegal?”

“Not that I know of. Besides, the police will be in by 2PM and we’ll be done by then. We’re not touching anything. Touching the crime scene may be illegal, but no one said we couldn’t take pictures.” She shows him a camera. “This camera’s my main investigative tool.” Handing him another camera, she continues. “I bought one for you.”

“What’re we doing with the cameras?”

“There’s enough film in these cameras for 400 photos. We’re going to take pictures of every surface of the kitchen. Since that’s where the crime possibly took place.”

“You really know your stuff.”

“I’m trying. Let’s go.”

They exit the vehicle.

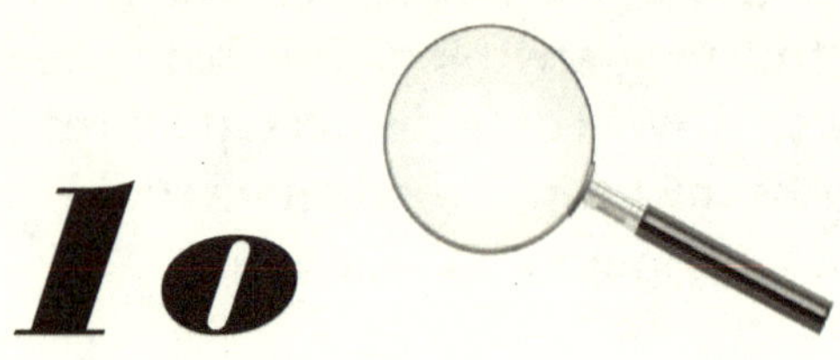

Chapter 10

Mayleigh lifts her head when the door opens. "Akio, you're here early."

"I have work later. How are you doing?" He sits on a chair.

"I'm good, missing my diner."

"How are you so calm in spite of what has happened to you?"

"I think about what they did to Jesus. Accusations, crown of thorns, pierced HIS sides, and then finally they hung HIM on a cross. And HE was innocent. But, after all that, Jesus was still able to tell a repentant thief

'Verily I say unto thee, Today shalt thou be with me in paradise.'
Luke 23:43

If an innocent man like Jesus could forgive those who persecuted HIM... The story didn't end there; the same Jesus who they killed *rose again* three days later and is on HIS throne.

As Christians we will always win, because God is in charge. Not man. There is purpose in the pain. Jesus' purpose was to save mankind. I know there is a reason that I am in here. I don't know what it is, but I trust God."

Akio smiles at her. "I admire your positivity."

"What about you? How are you holding up?"

"I'm reading the Bible more and gaining some understanding of the passages, but to be honest I can't focus. This thing with Nhyira is getting to me."

"I know that you love her and I believe things will work out. Even if she isn't your wife, you will find a woman who's beautiful and on the same path as you."

"That *sounds* nice, but I need to get her out of my mind. She's etched in my heart."

"I get it. I once had that with my husband."

"Do you think you'll ever get married again?"

"Who me? No," she chuckles. "I'm an old woman. That's not even in my thoughts."

Akio laughs. "You're not old Mayleigh, and any man who finds you will be a happy man."

"You're too kind."

He looks at his watch. "I gotta go now."

"Thanks for checking on me," she smiles.

"You're welcome. See you soon."

Mayleigh laughs. "It's not like I have anywhere to go…"

Chapter

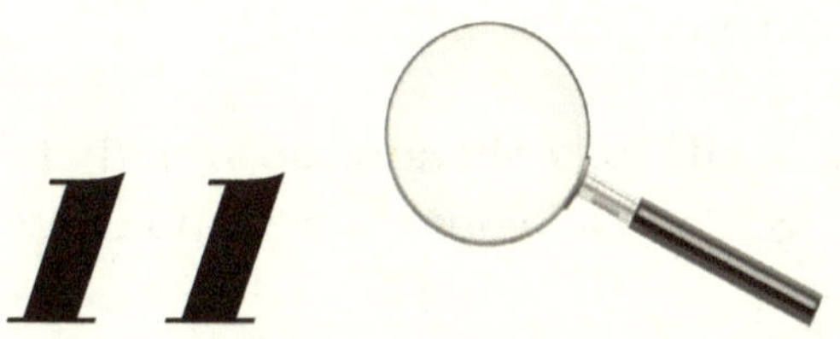

T wo hours later, Nhyira and Jörn enter the jailhouse.

"You're such a good friend to Mayleigh," he compliments.

"I appreciate your kind words. Not something I hear often."

"Determination is written all over your face. A quality I want in my future wife."

Nhyira coughs loudly. "Can we not talk about that now?"

"I was only making a comment."

"If it isn't Akio Qvareli," Jörn announces loathingly, when they arrive inside the building.

"I see you remembered my name. The festival is over, why are you still here?" Akio scoffs.

"Didn't know you were in charge of my life. Why is my presence such a bother to you?"

"What is going on between you and Nhyira?"

Jörn lets out a slight laugh. "My relationship with that wonderful woman is none of your business. You had your chance and blew it. Now it's time for a **real** man to step up."

Akio turns around. "I don't see anyone."

"Look here you small town boy, Nhyira is my woman and if you know what's good for you, you'd stay away from her. She loves me and we're getting married."

"Married?"

Jörn nods. "Not that it's any of your business, but I plan on proposing to her soon."

"I thought she wasn't interested in dating?"

"She didn't want to date **you**." He pokes Akio's chest. "Isn't it obvious? If you and Nhyira were meant to be together, you'd have been together. Too bad you didn't recognize her worth."

Akio bites his tongue to avoid saying something he'd regret later. Although he wanted to be the bigger man, inside he was provoked. He couldn't allow this man to get under his skin.

"We're happy together," Jörn continues, "so stay away from her and out of our relationship."

Akio enters his vehicle to pray.

> *"Jesus, You know how much I love Nhyira. Please help me to deal with it. I don't want to love someone or invest feelings and emotions in a woman who doesn't love You. You know the beginning from the end, so I pray that You help me to guide my thoughts. Remove all traces of jealousy that resides within me. Help me to respect her relationship with that man, even though it* ***upsets*** *me to my core. Please, please help me not to be angry at them. I commit my heart to You. I want to save my heart for the woman You have for me. Even though honestly I want it to be Nhyira, I know Your plans are greater than mine. Thank You for listening to me. In Jesus' name, Amen."*

"I thought I saw Akio," Nhyira states, when she returns from talking to the receptionist.

"He left," Jörn retorts. "Did you want to talk to him?"

"No big deal, I just thought we were cool."

"Evidently you're both on different pages. Anyway, I don't want to speak about him."

"I'm heading in to see Mayleigh. I don't know how she does it, but the woman's unruffled."

"You're a great support system to have."

Nhyira blushes.

Jörn's phone rings and he goes to answer it.

Moments later he shares the details of the call with Nhyira. "I'm sorry, but it looks like I have to head back home now. My boss wants to discuss something with me, but I have to be there in person."

"That's no problem. Your work is important. What you do is important. I'm grateful for the time you spent."

"I have a question to ask before I leave..."

Chapter

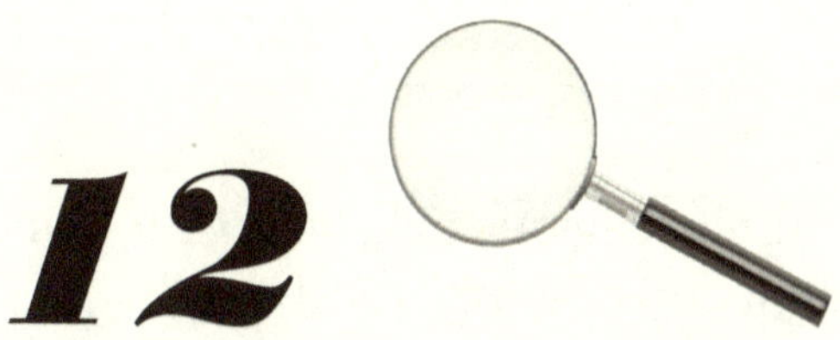

After Jörn's hasty departure, Nhyira enters the cell to see Mayleigh.

"Where's your friend?"

"He went back home; emergency meeting."

"Are you two an item?"

"Yes, we're in a relationship," Nhyira confesses.

"Do you love him?"

"Love grows. I'll grow to love him. We're good together. I know his family, he knew mine. What's stopping us?"

"I just think you're moving too fast and he may not be God's will for your life."

"I didn't come here to talk about your God," Nhyira scoffs.

"I'm only sharing what I feel led to share."

"While I appreciate and respect your beliefs, I'm not interested. We need to focus on the task at hand."

"You're in my prayers so I'm not worried."

Nhyira ignores Mayleigh's religious talk. "I have the photos from the crime scene. I was up all night and nothing stood out."

"Sure you weren't tired or distracted?"

"I've been doing this for a long time, nothing distracts me."

"I know you'll figure things out. I'm praying that God guides you to the right clues."

"There you go again. Just gotta slip that in huh?"

"Nhyira, I know you do not believe in God, but I do. And I'm praying that HE guides you."

"What you need to do Mayleigh," Nhyira emphasizes, "is pray that your God gets you out of here. Don't you want freedom?"

"You think being in here makes me a prisoner? No. I'm already free. There's a purpose for my imprisonment."

"Are you hearing yourself?"

"Loud and clear."

"What can be the reason for you being accused of a crime you didn't commit? The reason you've been sitting in jail for days?"

"When I know I'll tell you; but, I'm not afraid."

"I don't have time to decipher the battles in your mind. My goal is to get you out of here."

"And you will. You'll need God's help though. You can't do this on your own."

"I solved my uncle's murder on my own."

"You **think** you did. The gift that you have of solving and seeing beyond a situation, you think that's natural?" Mayleigh asks.

"I worked hard to get to where I am. I'd appreciate it if you stop downplaying my hard work."

"I'm not going to argue with you. But sweetie, you'll find your way to Jesus. That's my prayer."

Nhyira begins to feel uncomfortable in her chair. "I think it's time for me to leave."

"Before you go, I have a favor to ask. I know you've already done so much for me, but—"

"Whatever it is, I'll do it."

"You didn't even hear what it is," Mayleigh replies.

"You're a rational woman. I trust you."

"I trust you too. That's why what I'm about to ask, I don't trust anyone else to do."

"Ask away."

"Abacus has been visiting me in jail since my arrest. I've asked him to manage the diner while I await my trial. Would you consider working alongside him to run the diner? You're an excellent cook and organizer. He needs assistance."

"That's a tall order."

"No pun intended right?" Mayleigh laughs.

"What pun?"

"Some 'English major' you are. Can you help or not?"

"Never worked in a diner before, but sure I've got time in between writing."

"You'll do it?"

"Yes. I'll work at the diner."

Mayleigh smiles, "Thank you Nhyira. Thank you."

Chapter 13

The following morning Nhyira searched her closet for proper work clothing. She settled on a basic ***I ♡ Grape Fjord*** tee and jeans. If she was working with grease and food, she didn't want to mess up her good clothes.

"Come in, come in. Let me show you the kitchen and where you'll be working," Abacus greets Nhyira, when she arrives.

"Do you think Mayleigh made the right decision?"

"She's a good judge of character. Don't be nervous, you'll do well. You're already overqualified. Relax. You're too tense. One of the first things about working at this diner… You must be *relaxed*."

"Relaxed," Nhyira repeats nervously.

Breathe Nhyira breathe. You can do this.

Abacus puts on his chef jacket. "First, I'll introduce you to the team and we can get started on this morning's prep."

Nhyira's watch read **5:30AM**. She didn't know how the workers came to work each morning at 5AM after closing the diner at 10PM. Stretching out her tiredness, she follows Abacus to the kitchen.

The 6AM breakfast rush came and went before Nhyira could even blink. It was now time for the lunch patrons.

A group of boisterous individuals enters the diner.

"You Mayleigh?" one of the men asks her.

"No, my name's Nhyira."

The man's eyes widen. "You're THE NHYIRA ENOSIS? *Grape Fjord's Unscrambler/Njapa's Crime Solver*?"

"Who are you? Why do you know so much about me?"

"We're from out of town," the man announces. "Came to visit the ***scene of the crime***."

"Look buddy," Nhyira scolds, "We're not looking for any trouble. If that's your middle name, please leave now before I call the police."

"Whatever did I do?" He turns to his band of misfits and they all snicker.

Nhyira picks up the phone, indicating that she would call law enforcement.

The man places his hand on Nhyira's and she pulls away. "Come on pretty lady, that's not necessary. We were just leaving. We only wanted to see the crime scene. We'd never eat in this dump." He motions for the group to exit the diner.

Nhyira lets out a sigh of relief.

"Who was that? Are you okay? I heard a commotion."

"I'm okay, Abacus. They were just curious about the murder."

"Did you call the police?"

"No need to. I'm not scared."

"Nhyira, you're not invincible. Please don't do that again. I wouldn't know what I'd tell Mayleigh if something were to happen to you."

"I'll be fine."

"Take this to that lady over there." He hands her a steaming bowl of soup.

An hour later, a boy comes up to Nhyira, franticly. "Miss, miss, why do you have that sign in front your diner?"

Nhyira glances at him nonchalantly. "Did you want something? No freebies today."

"That means you didn't see. Come look outside," the boy pulls Nhyira. "There. Look." He points to the graffiti on the storefront.

AVOID THIS DINER.
DEATH IS SERVED HERE.

Nhyira holds her head in exasperation; knowing that the man with his rebel crew spray painted this horrendous sign in front of the diner.

No wonder no one's been coming in.

"Can you give me a description of the perpetrator?" Officer Zevallos requests when he arrives at the diner four minutes later.

"Medium built, about 5'8, he was wearing an oversized maroon tee, dark brown hair, green eyes, raspy voice, reeked of alcohol, and had a scorpion tattoo on the right side of his neck, you can't miss him," Nhyira rattles off.

The officer looks at her. "This is the most description I've gotten in my entire career."

"Nhyira's the best. She can solve any crime," Abacus chimes.

"Ever considered a job in law enforcement?" Officer Zevallos inquires.

"I'm sticking to writing," Nhyira retorts.

Officer Zevallos turns to Abacus. "You've worked with Mayleigh for a while right?"

"Since she started running the place, I'm the Executive Chef."

"Do you know of anyone who'd want to hurt her? Does she have enemies?"

"Her diner is the most popular restaurant in town. I can't think of anyone who'd hate her. In fact, the other restaurateurs dine here from time to time. Do you need anything else officer? We have customers," Abacus points out.

"That's all for now." Officer Zevallos turns to Nhyira. "I need you to come in for a statement."

"Sure. No problem," she nods.

"In the meantime, I'll send a team over to remove the graffiti. I can't have anyone messing up Mayleigh's Diner." Officer Zevallos strolls to his squad car.

What was that about? Does he like her? Hehe. I think Mr. Officer has a crush...

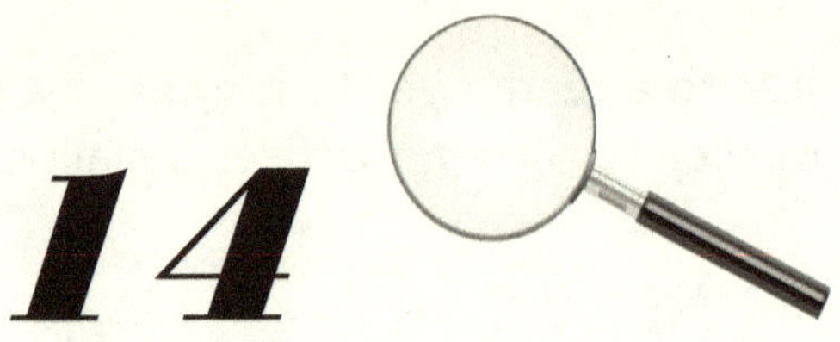

Chapter 14

N*hyira* picks up the morning paper and decides to take a gander at the headline news. To her dismay, her best friend's name was plastered all over the front page for the entire world to see...

The Echo Journal

MURDER AT MAYLEIGH'S DINER

May 26, 2000

Mayleigh's Diner: a place of food, fun, and **murder***. 42 year old Njapa native, Mayleigh Antao, has been arrested on first degree murder charges for the murder of Starr Island's top restaurateur and food critic, Cyprian Iwai.*

According to witnesses, on the night of Njapa's Chocolate Festival, Cyprian choked on Mayleigh's famous Plumberry Pancakes.

Another witness, who tried to perform CPR, noted that Mr. Iwai was dead.

The coroner has ruled the death as a homicide via poisoning. Reports show that the weapon of choice was ***Brorfliete****.*

Officer Zevallos, the first officer on the scene has denied comments. Mayleigh has also denied comments.

Regular patrons at the diner have stated that they would ***no longer eat at the diner****; for fear that they would also be a victim.*

Further details will be released to the public as information is made available.

In the meantime, the mayor has asked that anyone with information come forward.

BY: LEGEND GOLD

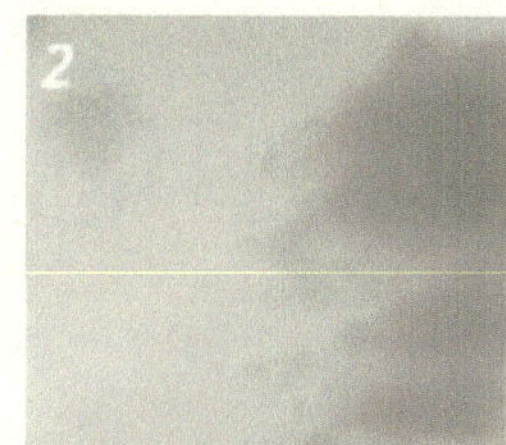

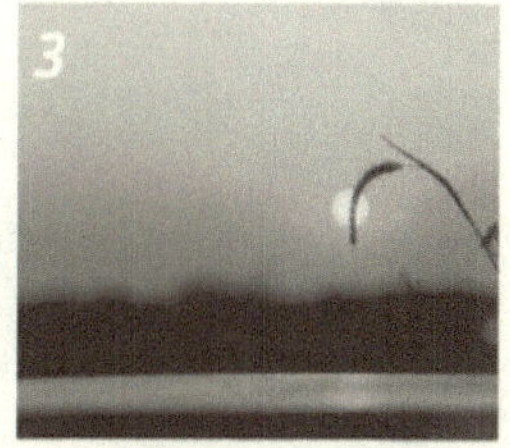

Don't forget to submit your Njapa Chocolate Festival pictures to be featured in next week's ***FUN PAGE****.*

THE ECHO JOURNAL | 1 *TEJ - SI*

Chapter

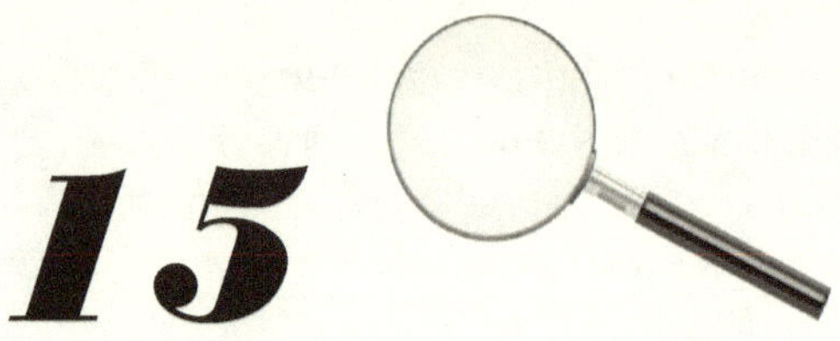

S*itting* in her library chair, Nhyira types **Brorfliete** in the search engine.

> *"Brorfliete is an unscented disinfectant created in 1978 and discontinued last year in Starr Islands. The disinfectant - once thought of as a milestone for parents seeking an alternative to the heavily scented disinfectants already on the market - was removed from shelves when an unidentified man accidentally swallowed the substance and died." The article read.*

Nhyira begins to tap on the computer table, thinking aloud. "Hmmm. *Unscented disinfectant. A restaurant kitchen. Only discontinued last year.* Think Nhyira think... Anyone who had access to it would've had to buy it in large quantities before it was removed... "

Nhyira pulls out her case files notebook.

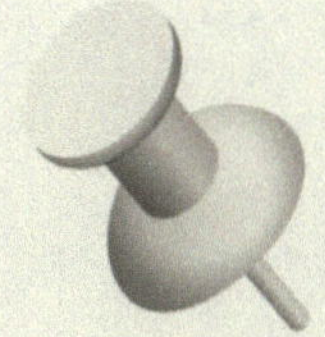

Case No: 2
Entry 1

NHYIRA ENOSIS

DETECTIVE

CRIME

A Starr Islands food critic poisoned with a banned disinfectant at Mayleigh's Diner.

SUSPECTED MURDERER

Mayleigh Antao

DECEASED

Cyprian Iwai

CONNECTION TO THE DECEASED

Diner owner being reviewed for an article.

LOCATION OF MURDER

Mayleigh's Diner

WEAPON

Brorfliete

MY NOTES

MAYLEIGH ANTAO

Owner of diner and citizen of Njapa. Friendly. Loving. No one has any complaints about her.

POSSIBLE SUSPECTS: *????*

~~*Mayleigh Antao*~~

- *She was the only person in the kitchen at the time of the critic's murder.*
- *Insisted that she make the batch of Plumberry Pancakes for the food critic.*

MOTIVE: She wanted a good review. Knew the deceased prior to that night????????

FOLLOW UP

Ask Mayleigh if she used Brorfliete even though it was banned.

Chapter 16

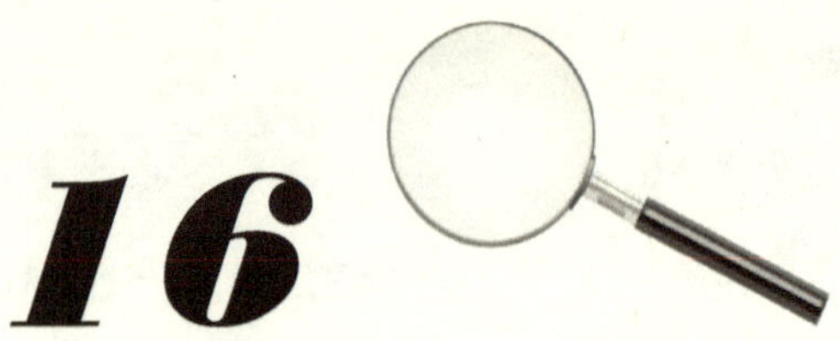

Putting down the newspaper, Officer Zevallos makes his way to Mayleigh's cell.

"How are you today?"

Looking up at the officer, she smiles. "I'm great. A little tired, but—"

"I have a question."

"Okay."

"How is it that you are able to remain composed after being indicted?"

"You don't think I did it?"

"I don't know. We haven't gotten all the facts."

"I'm innocent so therefore I have no reason to panic. I know justice will be served. There's purpose in my imprisonment."

"Sounds like something a Christian would say," he chuckles.

"I **am** a Christian," Mayleigh replies, proudly.

Officer Zevallos smiles, "Really?"

"Not ashamed to say it. I don't know if you're a believer Officer Zev—"

"Call me Hesiquio."

"I respect your office, sir... As I was saying, I don't know if you're a believer, but the God I serve will vindicate me. I have no worries. Why are you smiling?"

"I am too."

"*Too* what?"

"My apologies, I meant to say that I am a believer as well."

"Good to know, officer. Then you can understand why I am calm."

"You've been in here for almost a week and I've only seen you smile; like you're happy to be in here."

"No one's ever happy to be locked up, but I know there's no point in causing drama while the justice system works out the kinks. My lawyer, Jesus Christ, already knows what's going to come of this. Therefore, I'm sitting back and watching what HE does. In the meantime, I won't stop praying and praising."

"A woman of prayer huh?"

"What about you? Are you a man of prayer?" Mayleigh pauses. When did she become interested in the officer's private life?

"I do pray and I am getting to know Jesus. I learn something new every day reading HIS word."

"That's wonderful to hear. Your wife must be—"

"Mayleigh, Mayleigh. I have something for you to read," Nhyira interrupts. She stares at Officer Zevallos. "Can I speak to Mayleigh in private please?"

Officer Zevallos nods. "Yes, of course." He exits the cell.

Nhyira glances at Mayleigh. "What was that about?"

"N-Nothing," Mayleigh replies blankly.

"Mayleigh, what's going on?"

"Nhyira... I said... Nothing."

"Alright, but I don't know who you think you're fooling..."

Chapter

17

"**W*hat*** did you find out?"

Nhyira hands Mayleigh the article.

"What is this?"

"You have to read it."

"Oh."

"You seem distracted."

"I'm not." Mayleigh glances at the article then back to Nhyira. "Brorfliete? Wasn't that banned last year?"

"I hate to be the one to ask you this, but do you use that disinfectant, even though it's forbidden?"

Mayleigh chuckles lightly. "Oh, you're being serious?"

"This is no laughing matter. Just tell me. I need to know how to help you. Do you use the substance?"

"No Nhyira. I stopped using it the moment it was banned."

"I see."

"Wait a minute; do you honestly think I killed the food critic?"

"People are capable of anything with the right motive."

"Wow, this is coming from my best friend."

"I'm sorry, I had to ask. I know you're innocent, but I still need to ask. A detective isn't biased."

"Whew. I thought for a moment you were accusing me."

"Then how did the disinfectant end up in your batter?"

"I don't know," Mayleigh shrugs. "I used new ingredients; unopened packages. All of my workers know the diner's policy against Brorfliete."

"Can you see why you're the prime suspect?"

"It's unfortunate. Since everyone knows I kicked the staff out of the kitchen that night."

"Yeah. But, don't you worry; I'll get to the bottom of this. Or my name isn't **Nhyira Enosis**."

"I know that face. What is it?"

"Did you hire extra help for the festival?"

"My workers are capable of handling any event; large or small."

"Did you know Mr. Iwai before he came to your diner?" Nhyira rattles.

"We only corresponded briefly online concerning his review. But, I never met the guy. Were you thinking a jealous wife?"

"Look at you thinking outside of the box," Nhyira grins. "You don't know him so... Hmmmm. Think Nhyira think. The only logical explanation is that you've been set up."

"What's the motive?"

"That's what I can't figure out. I mean there were many guests in the diner. Who's to say that someone didn't slip something in his drink or- OR- hear me out... Someone slipped something into the pancakes while he was talking to other patrons. I mean he did have many people around him. Anyone could've done it and no one suspect anything. Nah, as I say it, it doesn't make any sense... Still doesn't explain the Brorfliete."

"It's okay hun. I know you'll figure it out. Go home, relax and then try again tomorrow. If I think of something I'll let you know."

"That sounds like a good idea. I am pretty beat. I don't know how you work at that diner every day for all those hours."

"It's not work to me. That diner's my home. I enjoy it."

Nhyira smiles at her friend. "You'll be back in there soon, don't worry."

"How's Abacus treating you?"

"He's the best; a good teacher and really kind to the staff."

"He really is a great worker and friend. Anyway, you should get going."

Nhyira hugs Mayleigh. "I'll be back."

Chapter

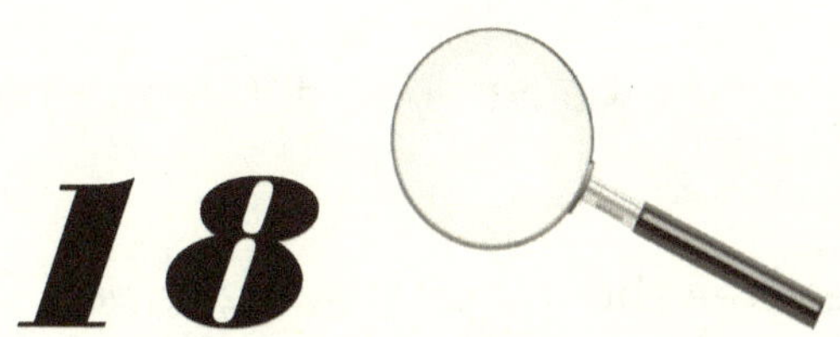

The second Nhyira exits the cell, Hesiquio enters.

"You're back, officer?" Mayleigh blushes.

He hands her a cup of *Cobalt Tea*. "Call me Hesiquio, please."

"I don't think so." She takes the cup from his hand. "Thanks. So wh—"

"We didn't get to finish our conversation and I'd really like to."

"I'm not sure what you're trying to accomplish here, but I'm in jail and I don't know for how long."

"I just want to talk that's all." He pulls up a chair.

"Okay then," she looks at him side eyed.

"You married?"

"You're just gonna jump right in aren't you?"

"Getting the tough questions out of the way."

"What if I was, would you still want to talk to me?"

Hesiquio hesitates. "It would be different. I respect people's relationships."

"Is that what this tea is all about? You *showing respect*?"

"I promise, I didn't mean anything by it. If you have a husband, I am sorry. I'm usually good at picking up signs."

"Signs? You know me all but a week. What are you—"

"Forget it. I just thought... " He proceeds to exit the room.

"Is that how you talk to women? By leaving when things get awkward?"

"Is it?" He lowers his gaze. "Awkward I mean?"

"I guess you haven't done this in a while."

"No," Hesiquio chuckles.

"Me neither. But by way of notice, if I was married, my husband would've been here. Believe me."

"So you're not married?"

"Widow."

"Another thing we share in common."

"You're a widow?" she laughs.

"I lost my wife twelve years ago. When did you lose your husband?"

"Five."

"Do you have any children?"

Mayleigh's face drops.

"Oh I'm sorry, did I say something to offend you?"

"No, no children," she exhales. "What about you?"

"I have a son, Miró. He's 14."

"You've been raising him all by yourself?"

"I do what I have to," he replies.

"I'm sure he appreciates it."

Hesiquio smiles. "I wish we would've met under different circumstances."

"Why? This is an interesting story. I'm sure my friend can write about it in a book someday."

"You know an author?"

"Nhyira."

"Interesting lady."

"She's a darling. How come I've never seen you around the diner?"

"We recently moved here from St. Jannaio."

"Never been."

"It's a lovely country. I hope you get to experience it one day."

"If I ever leave this place," she whispers.

He places his hand on her shoulder. "You will. We'll pray about it."

"Um. Yeah. Okay. Thanks," she moves her shoulder from underneath his hand.

"Well Mayleigh. I gotta go. I'll see you around."

"I have nowhere else to be."

They both laugh.

Mayleigh kneels down in her jail cell.

> *"Dear Lord Jesus,* **HELP**. *I pray that you will help me get out of jail. I'm 42 years old and have never been in trouble with the law; didn't even get punished during my school days. Why am I in here? I want to go back to work. I miss Bible Study, my friends. Please Lord; let me know the reason for this imprisonment. And also... Hmmmm. That man, your son, the officer. Hesiquio. I mean Officer Zevallos. I don't know what's happening with him or if this is a game to him, but please, yeah, I can't hide anything from You... I'm beginning to have these thoughts about him that I do not understand. The last man I loved is gone. I don't want to go through this again. So please, take away any thoughts I have for the officer. Amen."*

Immediately after her prayer, Mayleigh falls asleep on the floor.

Chapter 19

A few days passed since Nhyira last had her morning run. Being preoccupied with solving Mayleigh's case, she didn't have time for anything else. Thankfully, her aunt enjoyed cooking and ensured she got her daily nutrition.

Ever since his move to *Kanomatton*, there was no reason for Akio to be in *Njapa*, yet here he was running towards her. Although she was attracted to him and even liked him at some point, his current status in her life was **nuisance**. He didn't seem to get the hint that she wasn't interested in communicating with him.

"Good day Nhyira."

"Akio," she greets, continuing to run.

"Aren't you going to slow down?"

"What for?"

"We're having a conversation."

"We're not having anything. You can talk to yourself."

Akio stops in front of her, resulting in a bodily collision.

"UGGH! What do you want? Gosh."

"Did I say something to upset you?"

"I don't want to talk to you. You're annoying. Don't you get it?"

"I just wanted to see how you were doing," he responds, through the pain in his heart. It hurt him that the woman he loved, rejected him.

"I'm good, anything else?"

"Where's your friend?"

"Not that it's any of your business, but Jörn's back home. He **works**; which apparently you don't, since you're *always* in *Njapa*."

"Checking up on me are you? I have a day off so I came to run."

"Dude, I really don't care what you're doing with your spare time. I just want to run in peace."

"When did we become ***this***?" He mimics the tension between them.

"You're the one who stopped communicating with me."

"It was a poor choice on my part, but I have a valid explanation."

"One that I **DO NOT** care to hear."

"How's the investigation going?" Akio probes, ignoring her obvious irritation.

"It's going well. I am making progress. Mayleigh will soon be out. You could go ask her yourself."

"I'm asking you."

"Don't you have someone else to bother? Get a hobby. Clearly your life's boring, since you're so preoccupied with mine."

"Don't flatter yourself. I'm only asking about Mayleigh."

"Whatever you say, I don't care."

"You have a gift Nhyira. That gift comes from God. I pray that you continue to use it for good."

"I worked hard after my parents died to reach this stage in my life. No one else is getting credit for **MY** hard work."

"One day you'll see it. All that I've been saying is true. God loves you Nhyira and I—"

"You what? *Love me too*? Please. Spare me that foolishness. Go away. I don't want to see your face around here. I have a boyfriend and we're getting married."

Pacing her bedroom, Nhyira shakes her head in anguish. "Who does he think he is? The nerve of that man!"

Just then, her eyes fall on the stuffed white jaguar that Akio won for her two years ago at the chocolate festival.

"Why do I still have this?"

She picks up the bear and takes it to a closet in the hallway, burying it behind her uncle's antiques.

"He's not going to get to me. I need to donate that bear to charity; I have no need for it... "

Chapter

20

The following week, while exiting the grocery store, Nhyira bumps into Cyprian's irate wife.

"Watch where you're going!"

"Sorry ma'am."

"There's no **ma'am** here. We're practically the same age."

"Okay then." Nhyira rolls her eyes, noting that the woman was in her early 40s.

Delusional much?

"You're that sleuth girl aren't you?"

"If you're asking if my name is Nhyira Enosis, then yes I am."

"And you're helping the diner lady with her case?"

"Can I ask you a few questions about your husband?"

"I don't want to speak about the dead."

"It'll help me with the case."

"You think I care about you helping the woman who murdered my husband?"

"Mayleigh's not a murderer. Don't you want to know who the real killer is?"

Ziema lets out a snarky laugh. "I'm glad someone did what I wasn't strong enough to do."

"Mrs. Iwai, how could you say that? Someone killed your husband."

"What do you want me to do? Go on TV crying hysterically for them to bring his 'real killer' to justice? That scumbag deserved what came to him."

"Did something happen between you two?"

"It ***was*** happening, but no longer, since he's in an urn somewhere."

"You don't know where your husband's ashes are?"

"I told the mortician to do whatever he wants with it. But, I'm sure it's with one of his relatives. His parents will probably end up keeping it. I surely don't want it."

"But he was your husband."

"**Was** being the key word. We were in the midst of a divorce."

Nhyira stares at Ziema.

"Yes, that's right. The famous ***Cyprian Iwai*** was a lying cheat. Found that tidbit out four months ago. His mistress was his manager. Go figure. She ***managed*** him alright. When fame gets to your head, you think you're above the rules... " Ziema snaps.

"I'm sorry to hear that. No woman should experience a cheating husband."

"Word of advice: never get married."

"I've heard that a few times before, but all men aren't cheaters."

"That's what I thought."

"You should change your thought patterns then."

"I'm heading back to the hotel, if you'll excuse me." Ziema closes her car trunk.

Nhyira gulps loudly. Ziema's trunk contained a bottle of Brorfliete.

"You okay?" Ziema opens her car door.

"I-I'm fine," Nhyira stammers.

"All the best with your little investigation," Ziema quips.

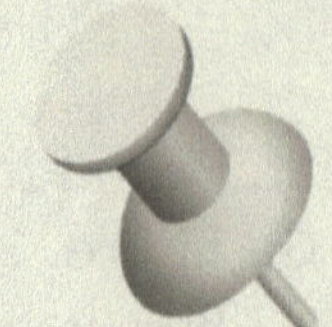

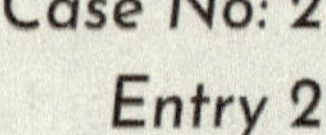

Case No: 2
Entry 2

NHYIRA ENOSIS

DETECTIVE

MY NOTES

Ziema Iwai: Wife of the deceased (MY NUMBER ONE SUSPECT)

MOTIVE

- *Angry that her husband was cheating on her.*
- *Impending divorce.*
- *Insurance money.*
- *Doesn't like his family.*

THOUGHTS

*Aunty Poet mentioned that the spouse is always the **obvious** suspect. Could Ziema fall in this category? Falsely accused because she is the **obvious** suspect.*

CLUES

- *Nonchalant attitude about her husband's death.*
- *Had a bottle of **Brorfliete** in her trunk.*

SUSPECT # 2

Cyprian's Manager.

- *Motive: Jealous mistress. Upset that her lover's divorce was taking too long????????*

FOLLOW UP

- *Do a background check on the Iwais. Find out if his cheating was made public.*
- *Who is his manager? Name? Did she make any comments in the news about his death?*
- *Did she gain anything financially from his death?*

Chapter

21

"**W***ho* are those people? What are they doing outside at 7AM?" Nhyira inquires.

Abacus continues his work. "Paparazzi. They've been in here asking questions. I've called the police on them and they went away, until the officers left."

"Maybe we should call them again. These people are messing up business."

"You can do that, I have work to do in the kitchen."

"You okay?"

"This is getting to me. My boss is sitting in jail for a crime she didn't commit."

"I know you care about Mayleigh."

"She's a good woman; doesn't deserve all this. Think you'll ever find out who did it?"

"You know I will. No matter how long it takes, I'll figure it out."

"That confident huh?"

"I was able to solve a 40 year old mystery. What would help though is getting surveillance cameras."

"*Njapa's* a quiet community; we have no need for those," Abacus replies.

"Well we do now. All these vandals and such, they need to be punished and we need evidence."

"Mayleigh's lucky to have a friend like you."

"I have to solve this crime, Mayleigh's my best friend."

"Abacus, can you come here for a minute? The stew burned," one of the sous chefs calls out.

"Duty calls, Nhyira. Handle your business out here." He runs into the kitchen.

He's such a dedicated chef.

Chapter

"**Good** day Officer Zevallos," Mayleigh blushes.

"Hesiquio. Please."

"It's weird calling you that; you're an officer of the law. I respect your position."

"Did you read the passage I suggested?" He points to the Bible he gave her the previous week.

"I did."

"What did you think?"

"Psalm 16, what a profound chapter."

"Did any verse stand out to you?"

"Verses 8 and 9, '***I have set the Lord always before me: because he is at my right hand, I shall not be moved. Therefore my heart is glad, and my glory rejoiceth: my flesh also shall rest in hope.***'"

"You can hope in God, Mayleigh."

"Amen."

"The chapter ends with the writer highlighting that in God's presence is *fulness of joy*."

"Thank you for encouraging me. Even though I know the scriptures, it's great to have encouragement from another believer."

"We'll keep having these Bible studies until you're out of jail."

"Why are you doing this?"

"I want to."

"There has to be another reason."

"I saw a need and I'm fulfilling it," Hesiquio replies.

"What need?"

"Encouraging you in the Lord."

"Officer Zevallos. You seem to be here more often than I am. Don't you have work to do?" Nhyira questions, when she sees him exit Mayleigh's cell.

"I am working," he replies, sauntering away.

Nhyira sits down on the chair opposite Mayleigh. "You want to tell me what's going on between you and the officer?"

Mayleigh begins to blush uncontrollably.

"Whoa, there **is** something going on."

"Nhyira, I don't know what's happening. I mean that night after the festival, he was abrasive. But since I've been in here, he's been nice. Like really nice. We even had a Bible study."

"Well, I know he's not trying to convert you since you're already a Christian. Could he be looking for a wife?"

Mayleigh covers her face.

"I love it. You like him. I can see that. And any man who visits you this frequently while you're **locked up** must like you too. That's more motivation for me to get you out of here. You can't be in a relationship with him behind a jail cell. Is your lawyer making any strides?"

"He's questioning the out of town guests. It's gonna take a while to track them all down."

"While he does that, I'll be busy solving this case."

"Got any more leads?"

"I had an interesting discussion with Mr. Iwai's wife. Apparently he was having an affair with his manager."

"An affair?"

"This gives me reason to mark his wife down as a suspect. She has motive, plus she doesn't seem to care that he's dead."

"That's your thinking face."

"It's just that... It seems too easily solved."

"Nhyira sweetie, everything in life isn't a puzzle. Sometimes the simple answer is **the** answer."

"I know, but I can't shake the feeling that I'm overlooking a pertinent clue. Also, I think there's something that Mrs. Iwai isn't telling me. For instance, why is she here and not with her family?"

"Everyone grieves differently," Mayleigh answers.

"That lady is not grieving."

"Are you sure you don't want to pursue a career as a PI? You're the best. You pay attention to the details."

"I enjoy my life as an author; simple and quiet. I don't want to be an investigator."

"Yet, here you are."

"It's not an everyday thing. Hopefully, this'll be my last case."

Mayleigh nods. "*Hopefully...*"

Chapter

23

W*hile* Nhyira dealt with her friend at the jailhouse, Jörn pulls up to the mansion.

Poet pauses from watering her flowers. “Jörn, it’s great to see you.”

“Can I help?” he offers.

“Sure,” she hands him a watering can.

“How have you been?”

“Is that a subtle way of asking for my niece?” Poet asks.

“I actually came here to see you.”

"Yeah right. How may I help you?"

"Let's go have a seat over there. It won't take long."

Poet wipes her hands on her sundress. "Oh, this is serious. Is everything alright?"

"Everything's fine," he answers. "I need to ask you something."

"I'm too old for you hun," Poet laughs.

"I see that you have a sense of humor."

"Come on, come on, out with it. I have gardening to finish."

"You are Nhyira's only living relative and I respect your bond."

"Uh huh... "

"I've loved your niece for a long time."

"Uh huh... "

"Can I have your niece's hand in marriage?"

Poet begins to scream excitedly. "You wanna marry my Nhyira? This is amazing. Yes, of course."

"So it's fine with you?"

"With me yes, but the decision's hers. You know I'm from the old school. I appreciate you coming to ask me, even though you don't have to. You're a good man."

"It's important to have the support of her family. Marriage is the union of two families and the start of a new one. Our children will be your nieces or nephews and I want to know you're on board from the onset."

"As I said before, the decision's all hers. But, welcome to the family, Jörn."

"Thank you Mrs. Veisiejai," he shakes her hand.

"You're welcome. Now if you'll excuse me, I have some gardening to finish."

"Go right ahead ma'am."

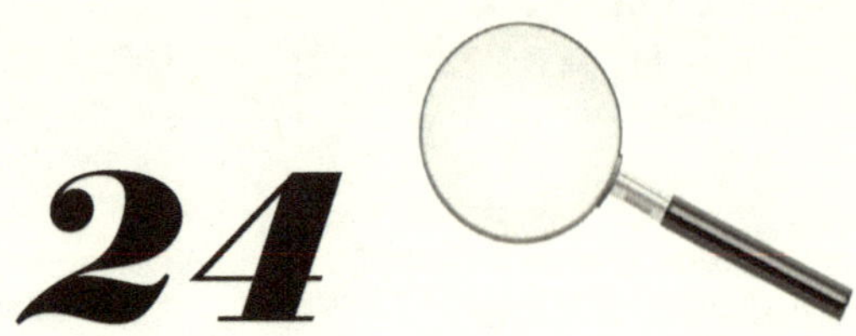

Chapter 24

"**Can** you come here for a minute?" Abacus calls to Nhyira during the lunch rush.

"Is everything alright?"

"I have a favor to ask."

"What is it?"

"I need you to make a delivery for me."

"Delivery? But, I'm needed here."

"Our deliver guy's out and I can't leave the kitchen."

"Where's it going?"

"The beach," Abacus reveals.

"A ***beach*** delivery?"

"Here's the exact location and the outfit that the person will be wearing," he continues.

"Name?"

"No name, just location and attire."

Nhyira squints her eyes. "I don't think I like this delivery idea, sounds fishy."

"It'll be fine." Abacus hands her the container.

Nhyira hesitantly stares at the person for the delivery. "Jörn?"

"You came. Good," he beams.

"The delivery's for you?"

"Yes."

"When did you come? Why didn't you tell me you were coming?"

"I wanted to surprise you."

"Well, I'm definitely surprised."

He embraces her. "I missed you."

"Me too," she giggles.

"I have something to ask you."

"Ask away. I'm all ears."

"Nhyira, you're a wonderful woman and any man would be lucky to have you in his life forever, but you've chosen to be with me and for that I am honored."

"Where are you going with this?"

Jörn kneels down and holds her left hand. "You're perfect for me and I don't want to go another day without making my feelings completely known. Will you marry me?"

Nhyira yanks her hand away and motions for him to stand. "Look Jörn, you're a nice man and I enjoy what we have, but I'm not ready to get married."

"It doesn't have to be now. I just want you to know how serious I am about us. No games."

"I know that you care for me, but can you give me some time?"

"I'm not taking this ring back. My great-grandmother gave it to me to propose to the woman I love and that's you. So please, wear it until you make up your mind."

"You're serious?"

"I am."

"Alright Jörn, I'll consider marrying you and I'll wear the ring in the meantime."

"I have another surprise for you," he says.

Isn't he full of surprises? I think I like it...

"This is a beautiful view. I've never done anything like this," Nhyira beams looking out the helicopter window. "*Njapa* looks more exquisite from this angle."

"I like the angle I'm seeing right here," Jörn kisses her cheek. "I think the world of you and I want to spend the rest of my life showing you that."

"You always know the right thing to say," she blushes.

"All the way over there is where we came from. Can you see your house?"

She squints into the night sky. "No."

"Me neither," Jörn chuckles.

Nhyira playfully punches his arm and he embraces her. Tipping her chin up to his mouth, he kisses her.

"I love you, Nhyira."

"I'm really sad you have to go back already."

"This was imperative for me to do. Now I can rest easy knowing that I have a fiancée waiting for me in *Njapa*."

"Almost-fiancée," Nhyira counters.

"I know you'll say yes."

Chapter

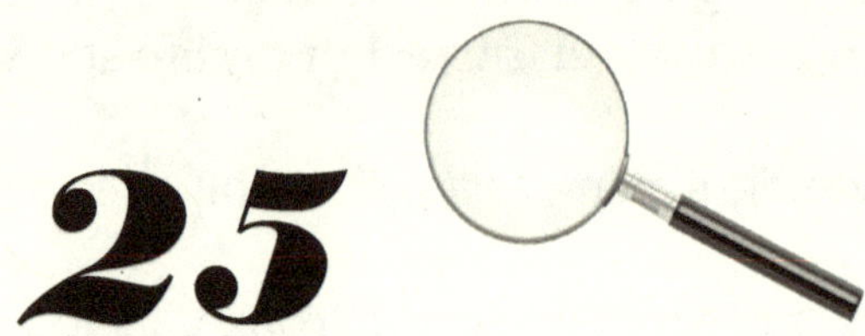

25

Being *almost-engaged* was a huge surprise for Nhyira. She hadn't expected Jörn to return to *Njapa* so soon. Now she had an 'almost-fiancé'. It didn't make any sense, but she was willing to try. Jörn was a good man who came from a reputable family. She had no reason to turn down his proposal.

"I'm happy to see— Uh, what's that on your finger?"

Nhyira flashes her ring, "An engagement ring."

"From who?"

"My boyfriend, I mean fiancé, Jörn."

Mayleigh shakes her head in shock. "I can't believe you're serious right now. A few weeks ago you didn't even want to be in a relationship. What changed?"

"When it's the right person you know. I'm still considering it."

"That means he isn't the right person."

"I'm still deciding if I want to be engaged at this point in my life. That doesn't mean Jörn isn't the right person for me."

"He isn't," Mayleigh replies. "Do you love him?"

"I respect him and he is a good man."

"That doesn't answer my question."

"I'm growing to—"

"You sound childish," Mayleigh scolds.

"I didn't come here for your judgment."

"No judgment here. I'm stating facts. Why would you accept the proposal of a man you don't love?"

"Love grows," Nhyira snaps. "I care about Jörn a great deal. He respects me. I know his family. They're good people. That's what matters to me."

"This is the most absurd thing I've heard you say in a long time."

"Shouldn't you be happy for me? I found someone who loves me. He wants to marry me."

"***Do you want to marry him*** is the question."

“YES!”

“Are you trying to convince me or yourself?” Mayleigh asks.

“I can’t do this with you right now. I came to share good news, but you’re ruining the moment,” Nhyira pushes back her chair.

“Oh, I’m sorry. I didn’t know you were in here,” Akio confesses.

“I was just leaving. Have a good day Mayleigh. I’ll come back someday soon.”

“You don’t have to go on my behalf,” he calls out.

“Let her go,” Mayleigh says. “She wants to leave.”

Chapter

A*kio* pulls up a chair. "What happened?"

"She didn't like what I had to say," Mayleigh shrugs.

"What were you speaking about?"

"A decision she has to make."

"Was that a ring I saw on her finger?"

"Yup."

"***Seriously?***"

"Yes," Mayleigh repeats.

"He proposed?"

"That's what an engagement ring on her finger means, Akio."

"I wasn't expecting that," he laments. "They've only just begun dating."

"According to Nhyira they've known one another forever."

"Does she love him?"

Mayleigh rolls her eyes. "That girl doesn't know what she wants."

"Yet, she's sporting a ring that **he** gave her."

"It's her life, we can't tell her how to live it."

"She's making a big mistake."

"That's not your concern."

"You know how I feel about her."

"And she knows how Jörn feels about her. It's not me who needs convincing."

"What am I thinking? I shouldn't even be considering Nhyira, she's not a believer."

"Her salvation is the most important thing. Not whether you end up with her or not. She's a soul that needs Jesus. You care about her, so we're going to pray."

Akio sighs heavily. "This is extreme. I was not expecting this."

"I know. I know. Don't be disheartened. You'll find the right woman."

Even though Akio knew Mayleigh was right, he didn't want another woman, he wanted Nhyira. Too bad being with her would ruin his relationship with Jesus. It was too late; she was engaged to another man.

He zones out of his conversation with Mayleigh, thinking about Nhyira. Snapping out of his thoughts, he scolds himself...

You need to focus Akio. Don't become consumed with her.

Chapter

27

O*pening* her house that night, Nhyira rubs her temples. She had too many decisions to make in such a short space of time.

What a day.

Loud cackles seep through the foyer from the kitchen.

Does aunty have company?

"Ms. Higüey? What are you doing here?"

"Good night child," Lively greets.

Nhyira stares in shock. “You’re in my house?”

“I am,” she nods.

“Why are you in my house?”

“I invited her,” Poet informs. “We’re having dinner.”

Shaking her head, Nhyira looks at her aunt and neighbor. “You’re having dinner with Ms. Higüey? What is happening in the world?”

“Did he do it?”

“Do what?” Nhyira asks Poet.

“Propose? Let me see the ring.”

“You knew about it?”

“Of course,” Poet nods. “He came and asked my permission.”

“You and Akio are finally going to tie the knot?” Lively quips.

Nhyira glares at Ms. Higüey. “Who said anything about Akio?”

“You’re seeing someone else?”

“He’s a friend of hers from back home,” Poet tells Lively. “His name is Jörn Oberhaus.”

“Fancy name, I’m surprised it’s not Akio. After all that trouble you gave me.”

“What trouble?”

“The noise. Late nights. Trouble,” Lively reflects.

"Ms. Higüey, I mean no disrespect, but are you losing it?"

"NHYIRA!" Poet snaps.

"What?" Nhyira rolls her eyes. "This woman has made my life miserable since the moment I moved here and she has the audacity to sit in my kitchen?"

Lively looks at Nhyira, "I sincerely apologize for the way that I treated you. You did nothing to deserve that treatment. Can you find it in your heart to forgive me?"

Nhyira glances at her aunt, who nods at her.

"Y-You're apologizing?" Nhyira gasps.

Lively nods, "Though I'm not proud to admit it, a lot of the things you have said are true; especially the one about respect."

Nhyira fans herself. "I need to sit down."

"Your aunt has taught me so much about forgiveness and being kind. I'm learning to be civil with my neighbors - humans in general. Poet's persistence has helped me," Lively reveals.

"I'm glad that you found a friend to confide in, Ms. Higüey," Nhyira smiles. "Apology accepted."

Poet claps in the background. "This is great. My niece and my friend are cordial with one another. Maybe one day we can all go on vacation together."

"I'd like that," Lively nods. "Get out of the old town."

"One day at a time Aunty Poet. I'm going to go lie down. A lot has happened today and I still have to solve Mayleigh's case."

"I want to hear all about your proposal," Poet adds.

Nhyira giggles. "I'll tell you later."

"I want to hear all about this Jörn fella, I really thought Akio was the man she'd marry," Lively adds, when Nhyira leaves.

"Well, Akio didn't know what he wanted. I'm happy my niece found herself someone who does..."

Chapter

N*hyira's* watch displayed **5AM** on the dot, yet the door to the diner was closed. Unbuckling her seatbelt, she makes her way to the entrance and knocks. Peering inside, she sees nothing but darkness.

What on earth is going on?

Just then, someone comes up from behind and startles her. "Abacus, you scared me."

"I'm sorry. What are you doing here? Isn't it your day off?"

"No, I'm working today."

"My apologies. That must've been another employee."

"What's wrong? Why's the diner closed?"

"I have to go out of town for a few days, family emergency."

"Is everything alright?"

"I wouldn't know until I get there. I really have to go, Nhyira."

"What about the diner?"

"Ask Mayleigh what to do," Abacus replies. "I didn't get a chance to speak with her. This just happened and I need to go now."

"Go handle your family business," Nhyira answers. "I'll let her know."

Abacus walks to his car. "Thanks. See you when I get back. Here are the keys in case you need anything."

"Do you know when you'll return?"

"No." He waves and closes the car door.

That was odd. I hope everything's alright.

"No work today," Nhyira cackles. "Guess I'll search the diner to see if I missed anything."

Chapter

29

"**Why** didn't I notice this before?" Nhyira looks over at Mayleigh's ajar locker.

In all of her snapshots, she hadn't paid attention to the open cabinet. She strides over and further opens the door.

"No. It can't be," she gasps.

Inside the locker was an enormous bottle of **Brorfliete**.

"This is not possible. Mayleigh lied to me? I didn't even know they had bottles that big."

Nhyira sits on a nearby stool, taking in the shock she'd just received.

She takes photos of the substance.

"*Anyone is capable of crime, with the right motive.* But what would be Mayleigh's motive? Why would she want the critic dead when he was writing a review for her diner?"

After her last experience with a criminal, she knew that some people lie without remorse.

Did Mayleigh lie to me? Why didn't I think of this before? What connection does she have with Mr. Iwai? None of this makes any sense.

Back at home, Nhyira researches all the cities that Mr. Iwai visited during his years as a food critic. All of her searches came up futile; he'd never been to Celgagoas prior to the festival. Even the ship logs from the harbormaster didn't have his name. Could *Cyprian Iwai* be an alias?

It wasn't unheard of.

The only logical explanation for this crime; it was an accident. Yet, deep down Nhyira knew that couldn't be true. This crime was premeditated and she was determined to expose the killer; even if it was her ***best friend***...

The ring stared up at Nhyira, reminding her that she had a decision to make. Was she really going to marry a man she didn't love? Was *growing to love* him enough? Although she hadn't contemplated marriage much in the past, she didn't want to settle for mediocrity.

Turning off her lamp, she falls asleep thinking of Akio.

Chapter 30

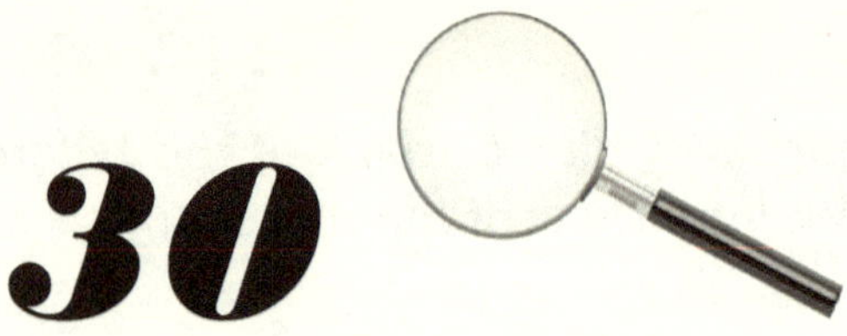

M*ayleigh's* heart leaps at the sight of Officer Zevallos. She didn't know when she took notice, but the man was handsome; he had a movie star face and the body of an athlete. Each day they spent together, she wondered why he visited so often. She'd never considered loving another man after her husband died, but the officer got her attention.

"I brought you dinner," he announces.

"Thanks." She stares at the container solemnly.

"I know it's not food from your restaurant, but it was the closest thing nearby; a newly opened restaurant. It's Trinidadian food. This is Bake and Shark."

"Shark you say?"

"You know Mrs. Denoble, the librarian? Well, her family owns the restaurant."

Mayleigh takes a bite of the sandwich. "This is incredible. I can't lie."

"They make excellent food. My son and I have been eating there all week."

"I guess my diner will get stiff competition."

"No competition," Hesiquio adds. "There's room in town for variety. And your customers love you."

"By the time I leave here, they may be regular patrons at the other restaurants," she scoffs.

"No negative thoughts. Trust God. You'll get out soon."

"How's your son?" Mayleigh asks.

"He's great. Speaking of my boy," he points to his ringing cell phone, "that's him calling. I'll be right back."

Mayleigh paces her cell.

Letting out a loud sigh, she prays.

> *"Jesus, please help me. I'm excited when he's here. Sad when he's not. When I'm around him I can barely contain myself. Your son is gorgeous and I don't know if I can do this. If he's not your will for my life, please remove him. Ain't nobody got time for that..."*

When she finished praying, she looks up to see Hesiquio staring at her while speaking on the phone. He waves to her and she waves back.

I can't do this again. I haven't dated in a long time. Plus I'm in jail. How would this work?

Chapter 31

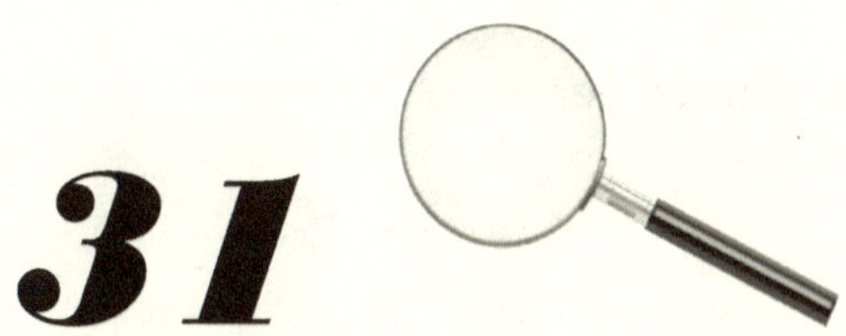

"**Night** my love," Jörn says into the receiver. "I haven't heard from you in a few days."

"I've been busy helping Mayleigh," Nhyira replies.

"Making any headway?"

"Sort of, I feel overwhelmed though."

"Then join me."

"Where?"

"I'll book a ticket for you for tomorrow: **Amethyst Island**. You need a vacation. I know that you've been working hard. I have an assignment there and I'd like for you to accompany me."

"This is a huge step. We've never been on vacation together."

"I want to help you in any way possible," Jörn responds.

"Let me think about it."

"No problem. I hope you say yes."

"You'd **better** say yes," Poet states, ten minutes after Nhyira hung up the phone. "That young man's respectful, considerate of your feelings **and** wellbeing. What else do you need?"

"So you don't think I'm crazy?"

"You staying in *Njapa* when you have an opportunity to go somewhere to clear your head is what'll be crazy. You've been working endlessly to help Mayleigh. Nothing's wrong with taking time for yourself."

"But she's still in jail."

"Go clear your head and then come back with a fresh perspective," Poets states.

Nhyira sighs. "Are you sure I'm not making a mistake?"

"Do you care about him?"

"Yes."

"Does he make you feel safe and wanted?"

"Yes."

"Then go."

"Alright then... I'm going to **Amethyst Island,**" Nhyira squeals.

"And Nhyira—"

"Yes aunty?"

"While you're at it, give that man an answer. He's only going to be patient for so long. Trust me."

As the sun rose the next morning, Nhyira looks out of the airplane window hoping that she was making the right decision.

Chapter 32

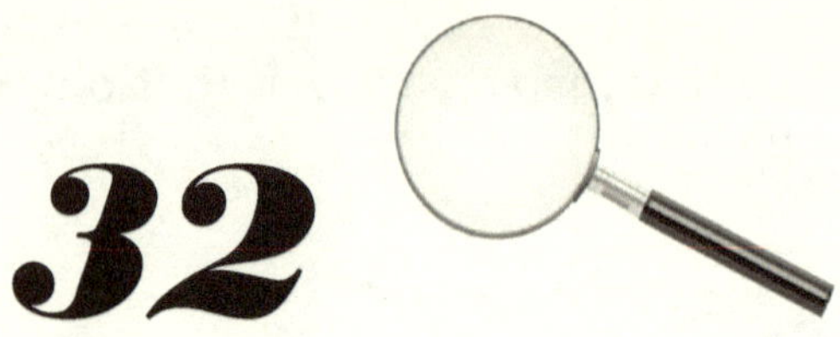

La Corazon, Amethyst Island

Nhyira shivers from the blast of the airport AC. Her sweater was located in the bottom of her suitcase. In the distance she spots Jörn holding up a jacket.

He thinks of everything.

Before she could blink he was embracing her.

"You're so beautiful. This is for you. The AC here is always on full blast."

"That was thoughtful of you," Nhyira smiles.

"I'm practicing."

"You're doing an excellent job."

"Let me get that for you." He rolls her suitcase out to the curbside.

"Yes," Nhyira calls out.

Jörn stares at her puzzled, while he placed her luggage into the trunk. "I didn't ask any question."

"Yes, I'll marry you," she adds excitedly.

Jörn beams and twirls Nhyira around.

Nhyira and Jörn gaze at the beautiful sunset. He had taken her to the water's edge to watch the sun go down. A tradition they'd started when he visited *Njapa* for the Chocolate Festival.

"I hope there'll be many more days like this."

"Me too," Nhyira giggles. "What did you want to talk to me about?"

"You want to talk about it now?"

"Why not?"

"I got a job offer at the palace in Voque as a nurse for the Royal Police Force."

"Look at you working with the elite. Being a nurse for the RPF can take you to places you never dreamed."

"We need to discuss a wedding date so that we can start our life together. I've already been looking at properties there."

"Whoa, slow your roll. I just said **yes**. Besides, I can't leave Aunty Poet behind."

"We can get a place for her near us. She doesn't have to stay in *Njapa*. I know how much she means to you."

"Wait a minute," Nhyira pauses. "Wait a minute. I'm happy for you, but do we have to talk about the future, ***now***?"

"Why do you always dodge the topic? Don't you want to marry me?"

"Yes, maybe one day, but not now."

"I thought all women dream of their wedding day and want a man to marry them as soon as possible."

"Not me. I want to take my time."

"You're talking as if you don't want to be with me," Jörn says.

Nhyira interlocks her fingers with his. "I do want to marry you. It's just that I've been living alone for so long... Give me time, I'll get there."

"No problem, my love. Let's get something to eat."

"How many in your party?"

"Two," Jörn tells the Maître D'.

"Right this way." The man escorts Nhyira and Jörn to a table.

Jörn pulls out the chair for Nhyira.

"Your waitress will be right with you," the man informs.

"This place is fancy." Nhyira places a napkin on her lap.

"Definitely not diner food," Jörn knocks.

"Watch it."

"I didn't mean anything."

"Mhmmm."

"How's your book coming along?" he asks.

"I've been so busy with this case I haven't even thought about the book."

"I'm sure your readers want more of your work. It's been over a year."

Nhyira raises her eyebrow. "I didn't know you were my book agent."

"I can be if you want me to."

"You don't know the first thing about the book world," Nhyira laughs. "Stay in the medical field."

Jörn takes a sip of water.

"Is that who I think it is?"

"Who?" Jörn follows her finger.

"Abacus."

"Abacus?"

"The Executive Chef from the diner," Nhyira adds.

"What is he doing here?"

"I don't know, but I'm going to find out."

"Nhyira **wait**!" Jörn yells.

Chapter 33

"**F*ancy*** running into you here."

Abacus looks up. "Nhyira?"

"I thought you had a family emergency?"

"I came to eat. Need to think. Why are you here?"

"I'm with my fiancé," she points to Jörn.

"You said yes?"

"Indeed."

"That's nice," Abacus nods.

"Are you here alone?"

"I am."

"You look sad. How's your family?"

"Coping."

"What happened?"

"My brother got into a car accident and is in critical condition at the hospital," Abacus shares.

"Can I come to the hospital with you; as a form of support?"

"Thanks Nhyira," Abacus replies. "I'm really surprised you'd do that."

"I'm sure if Mayleigh was here she'd do the same."

"How is she? I haven't gotten a chance to speak to her."

"She's hanging in there. I'm making progress on the case. But, I wouldn't bore you with the details. Your family's important."

"We can leave now if you want," Abacus states, summoning the waiter to bring his check.

"I'll go tell Jörn."

"Won't he be upset your date was cut short?"

"I don't see why he'd be upset," she shrugs.

Abacus talks to the nurse, while Nhyira waited for her turn to visit Abacus' brother. Although she didn't know him, she knew the importance of coworkers supporting one another. Abacus was old enough to be her father and she respected him.

"I think he likes you," Jörn whispers.

"Who?"

"Abacus."

"You're kidding," Nhyira scoffs. "Do you know how old he is?"

"Some men like younger women. You're of age, so why not?"

"Did you hit your head on your way in?"

"I saw how he was looking at you in the restaurant," Jörn mumbles.

"Is that why you were quiet on the way here?"

"Surprised you even noticed," he scoffs.

"I thought you just wanted silence. Sometimes I appreciate it too."

"No Nhyira, I didn't want silence. I couldn't get a word in edgewise. You were too busy yapping it away with Mr. ***Executive Chef*** over there."

"I-I... You're serious right now?"

"I'm a man, I can tell these things."

"I don't care who likes me. You have no right to tell me who to speak to. Abacus is a coworker. That's it. Whatever you **think** you're seeing, you need to get your eyes checked."

"My opinion doesn't matter? First Akio, now Abacus?"

"Are you always going to bring up Akio?"

"I know what I see," Jörn huffs.

"What is going on with you? Why are you talking like this?"

"You're not taking my feelings for you seriously, it makes me wonder sometimes."

"**Unbelievable**. I come all the way out here and you're making crazy accusations? I'm going. I'll take a cab back to the hotel. You have **some nerve,** Jörn."

Chapter

34

Maybe *coming here was a bad idea. It's never good to ignore one's instinct.*

Nhyira stares at the missed calls on her phone.

That man could kick rocks for all I care. Abacus likes me? Ha. What a joke. Even if he did, Jörn doesn't trust me.

She taps her fingers on the bedhead.

Is this what I have to look forward to in marriage; a husband who would accuse me because of his insecurity?

Jörn knocks on Nhyira's room door. "Open up Nhyira. Can we talk?"

"No. Go away!"

"I'm sorry."

Nhyira gets up from the bed and heads towards the door. Peering out, she asks, "Sorry for what?"

"For being a jerk, it's just that I love you so much and I know that men will want to be with you. Living apart from you is driving me crazy."

"Jörn, you can't go around making these accusations. I'm sure you have many women throwing themselves at you in the hospital, Mr. Male Nurse."

"So we agree that you need to move to Voque with me?"

"After we're married."

"That's all I want."

"Can I go to sleep now?"

"I'll see you in the morning." He kisses her forehead.

Chapter 35

The air was frigid that afternoon, but Akio needed to think. After his visit with Mayleigh, he decided to check on Nhyira. It'd been days since he saw her at the jailhouse. And with the diner being closed, he had no other way of seeing her.

Running through the park, he spots the Veisiejai House in the distance. Though he hadn't been there in a while, he trots over.

Mrs. Veisiejai was tending to her garden.

"Good afternoon ma'am."

Poet tilts her hat upward. "Hello Akio. How are you?"

"I'm good."

"What brings you by? Let me guess, my niece?"

"Is she around?"

"Not unless she came back early, she went out of the country with her fiancé."

"Fiancé?"

"Jörn."

"She made a decision?"

"She did," Poet nods.

"So she's going to marry him? Does she love him?"

"Don't do this to yourself, Akio. You seem like a nice young man. You'll find yourself someone special. My niece already made her choice."

"You're happy with her choice?"

"What's there not to be happy about? He's good looking, has a career, treats her well and she never has to question how he feels."

"Shots fired?"

"Is that a slang of sorts?" Poet asks.

"Are you insinuating that I didn't treat her well?"

"I don't dwell on the past. What happened between you and my niece is none of my business. She doesn't hate you, I know that much."

"But, she doesn't love me, right?"

"It's too late for that conversation. It'll be best for the both of you if you don't come around anymore. I don't want you confusing her."

"You're right. I shouldn't have come here. Enjoy the rest of your afternoon Mrs. Veisiejai."

Poet turns and continues to water her plants.

Akio leaves the area sullenly.

She's going marry him? This is ridiculous. Get a grip Akio. Nhyira's off limits for many reasons.

Chapter 36

Akio runs angrily into the park. He bumps into a woman. "Mrs. Iwai, I'm sorry. I didn't see you."

"I'm certainly not invisible," she rubs her arm.

"How have you been?"

"Couldn't be better."

"What are you still doing in *Njapa*?"

"I'm waiting for the trial to begin, so that I can personally thank Mayleigh."

"For what?"

"Killing Cyprian of course. She did what I wanted to do."

"I'm an officer; you shouldn't say those things around me."

"I don't care who you are. I'm free to speak my mind."

"Did you love your husband?"

"At one point yes," she shrugs. "But that all went downhill the more he got assignments around the world. I found out why a few months ago. *Mistress.*"

"He was cheating on you?"

"I guess a beautiful supportive wife wasn't what he wanted."

"This saddens me. No man should treat a woman like that."

"I don't need your pity. He got what he deserved."

"Forgive him so that you could be free."

"You think I'm not free? He's not around to humiliate me. I'm just happy this news didn't hit tabloids. The last thing I need to be is a spectacle. That was one thing his manager was capable of, keeping Cyprian's private life out of the media. You know we hardly have pictures together? Yet, they have tons of pictures. You'd think **she** was the wife. I was naïve."

"You trusted him," Akio adds. "That's what a wife should do."

"And a husband should **remain faithful,**" she yells indignantly.

"You are correct."

They continue conversing briefly about their backgrounds.

“You married?”

“Not yet,” Akio responds.

“It’s probably best if you don’t get married.”

“You’re only speaking out of hurt. Would you like me to pray with you?”

“No thanks. I’m fine,” Ziema taps his arm before she jogs away.

Chapter

"I have something to tell you and I don't know how you'll take it," Officer Zevallos announces.

Mayleigh braces herself, preparing for the worse. "Go ahead."

"I have strong feelings for you."

"You do?"

"Yes. I've known it for a while, but it has intensified."

"Oh officer, I have feelings for you too. However, it doesn't matter. I'm stuck in here. My trial has been pushed up to one month from today. We don't have a future together. I can't be with you from behind bars. I appreciate your company these past few weeks, but I can't. I'm sorry."

"I'll continue to pray that the charges are dropped against you and that the real killer is found."

"I've been thinking about that for a while. Maybe this is how I'm meant to spend the rest of my life."

"Come on Mayleigh, you can't honestly believe that," Hesiquio replies.

"Why not? My lawyer has no leads from his investigation."

"What about Nhyira?"

"Haven't seen her since last week."

"She probably took a break. This isn't an easy job and she isn't even an official."

"I'm not blaming her and she does deserve a break. I've been thinking that maybe I'm looking at this all wrong. My ministry is probably in jail/prison. I've been able to share my faith with the other inmates. It could be for the rest of my life. The diner is my past," Mayleigh sighs.

"I know you don't believe that. Prison ministry is a great thing, but you're not going to spend the rest of your life behind bars. We **have** to trust God that the charges will be dropped. We **must** pray that the truth will come out and you will be set free."

"All the evidence points to me; I was the only one present. There were no cameras. I have no alibi. How will this be solved with no evidence to exonerate me?"

"Keep your eyes on Jesus. Don't try to figure it out. Let us pray," Hesiquio offers.

Chapter

38

"**I'm** baaaacccck." Nhyira announces, placing her suitcase on the foyer stairs.

Poet hugs her niece. "How was it?"

"It had its good moments. I'm happy to be back in my home."

"Dinner's on the stove if you're hungry."

"I'm not hungry, but what's up with you?"

"I've been attending different activities at the library."

"That's awesome. I'm happy for you. What about Mayleigh, have you visited her?"

"Yes, I just came from the jailhouse."

"I hope she isn't mad I took a break."

"You're doing her a favor sweetie and she knows that. Her lawyer's been working extra hard as well."

"Any updates?"

"His quest to find out information from all the visitors came up empty. Her trial date's been moved up to next month."

"I thought we had until the end of the year?" Nhyira asks.

"That's the update," Poet shrugs.

"If I don't get her out soon, then I've failed."

"You're doing more than anyone expects."

"I can't shake the feeling that I'm missing something."

"Do you have any idea what that could be? Want me to help?" Poet bids.

"No, you stay focused on enjoying your freedom. I don't want you caught up in this system again, even if it's to help someone else."

"You'll solve it. I know you will."

Nhyira sighs.

"So, tell me about your trip."

"I really don't want to speak about it."

"Come on Nhyira. We haven't spoken about your relationship or wedding plans since you got engaged. What's going on?"

"I just have a lot on my mind that's all."

"I'm here for you, you know that."

"When I'm ready to discuss it I'll let you know."

"That's a brush off."

"Aunty, please..."

"Okay, if you say so. Don't let your dinner get cold."

"I won't. First, I'm going to take a shower, and then I'm going to brainstorm."

Chapter

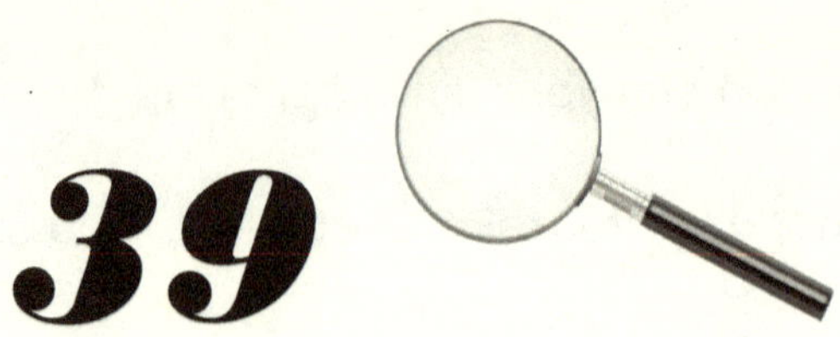

The weekend came and all Nhyira wanted to do was relax at the poolside. Walking towards the pool house, she stops.

What's this?

"Oh, there it is." Poet takes the book from Nhyira's hand.

"What is it?"

"A Bible, your uncle has tons in his library."

"Not you too. Mayleigh, Akio, now you. I don't want you to get caught up in religion. All we need is to live a good life."

"I started reading it with Lively when you weren't here. I'm intrigued by the contents."

"We've never discussed religion in this house. I know you believe in a higher power, but this... Why now?"

"It's not hurting anyone. And it's not a religious book. It's about love, relationships, truth, and forgiveness. There are so many topics. Like this one book I'm reading called *John*, talks about God loving us and giving HIS Son **Jesus** to die for our sins. If that isn't love then I don't know what is."

"You believe a father would give up his son to die for **other people's** bad choices?"

"Not just any father, **God**."

"Then you're just as delusional as Mayleigh. I love her, but she's been caught up in this cult for over a year."

"It's not a cult," Poet states. "No one's forcing us to do anything. We don't have to pay to join, nothing."

"Seems too good to be true for a man to die for other people's sins; no one's perfect and everyone should pay for their own wrongdoings."

"Jesus is perfect and HE **chose** to take on our sins, so we don't have to continue to live a life making wrong choices."

"Well, so long as you're not caught up in a cult you can do whatever you want aunty. Just don't bring any objects in this house."

"Oh no there's none of that. It's about a relationship with God. No need for any objects."

Nhyira rolls her eyes. "You're starting to sound crazy."

"You should read the book. You'd love reading this one. It's a good book."

"No thanks, I'll stick to the genres I like; nothing religious."

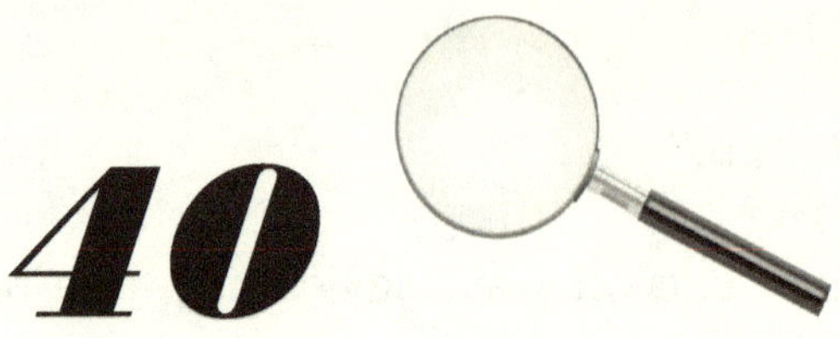

Chapter 40

Terganess, Kanomatton

A*kio* sat in his favorite restaurant swirling his stew in the bowl. The waiter places a glass of water on his table. However, Akio's mind was not on food. He thought back to the first time he'd met Nhyira.

"Wow, good night beautiful," Akio greets.

"Thanks Mayleigh. You were right. Those pancakes are delicious. I'll be back." Nhyira makes her way to the exit.

Not used to being ignored Akio stops Nhyira in her tracks. "Don't you have any manners?"

"Oh I'm sorry. I didn't notice you. I thought you were speaking to Mayleigh."

"That's Nhyira, she's new in town," Mayleigh informs him.

"Clearly. Not too friendly," he scoffs.

"Again, I'm sorry," Nhyira apologizes.

"Akio Qvareli," he declares, putting out his hand.

Nhyira opts out of the handshake, staring at the door she wanted to exit. "What?"

"My name in case you were wondering," Akio adds.

"Actually, I wasn't. Thanks again Mayleigh. See you later," she says, walking out of the diner.

He also reminisced on their time at her first Chocolate Festival and the night he'd help her break down a secret room in her house so she could help get her aunt out of prison.

For whatever reason, he couldn't stop thinking about her. No matter how much he prayed, the thoughts wouldn't go away.

Months ago, when he'd started attending church he stopped communicating with her. When an opportunity for him to move to *Kanomatton* permanently came, he took it.

It was a poor choice on his part not to tell Nhyira, but he knew she wouldn't understand why they could no longer date.

Now that he was confident to explain it to her, his chance was gone. She'd moved on and was engaged to be married.

That was the worst part in all of it; seeing her parading around town with another man. Although he knew one day his heart would be free to love another, he just wasn't ready to let Nhyira go.

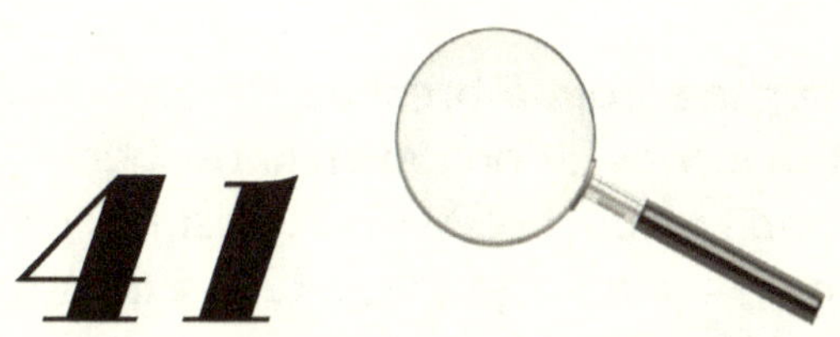

"**W*elcome*** back," Mayleigh greets.

"Are you mad?" Nhyira asks nervously.

"Why would I be mad?"

"Because I went away for a bit, I haven't been here for you."

"Nhyira, you've been visiting me consistently since I've been locked up. I think you deserved a break. Isn't that what you were doing?"

"My fiancé invited me on a vacation to relax and clear my head."

"Fiancé now, is it?"

"We're official. I said yes."

“No more contemplation?”

“I know what I want.”

“And you’re sure it’s him?” Mayleigh asks.

“Speaking about relationships, you didn’t tell me why you and Abacus never got together. You are such great friends and respect one another,” Nhyira prods.

“Abacus has been hurting from a breakup he had 10 years ago. He never told me who the woman was. I don’t even know her name. He doesn’t like to speak about her and I respect his wishes. Besides, I was happily married. When my husband died 5 years ago, it took me a long time to heal. I’m not fully over his death and I still miss him, but it hurts less now.”

“What about now? You’re both single.”

“We’re better off as friends. I like someone else.”

“Officer Zevallos?” Nhyira teases.

“Yes,” Mayleigh giggles.

“I think it’s cute. You two would make a wonderful couple. Too bad you met under these circumstances.”

“He said something similar.”

“I didn’t care for him much in the beginning. Real know-it-all type, but he’s grown on me. Any man that would visit you this much really cares for you. Have you shared how you feel?”

“We have.”

“Okay Mr. Officer,” Nhyira chuckles. “I see you’re working fast.”

"Stop that."

Nhyira laughs. "What? Just saying, you'd think he's coming in here to work. Apparently he's working on his flirt game. Don't think I haven't seen those exchanges between the two of you."

"I don't know what you mean, girl."

"Mhmmm. I bet you think about him a whole lot and you miss him when he's not here."

"I do," Mayleigh blushes.

"Marry him then."

"I can't marry anyone being stuck in here."

"Don't worry; you won't be in here forever. Maybe you came in here for your husband to ***find you***."

"Have you been reading the Bible?"

"Bible?" Nhyira scoffs. "I heard that on a TV show."

"That's Biblical."

"Oh, is it? Okay. Cool. Well anyway, you two would make a lovely couple. Let's wait and see what happens when you leave here."

"What about your wedding plans?"

"I haven't started yet."

"What are you waiting for?"

"I'm enjoying the engagement period," Nhyira counters. "We're young, no need to rush into it. Why can't we just enjoy our engagement? What's the hurry?"

"I agree with you. This is an important time in your life. I will tell you this though: if you truly love him you'd marry him tomorrow. That's how I felt with my husband."

"That's why no two stories are the same. It worked for you, but I won't be pressured into marriage."

"Are you feeling pressured?"

"I didn't say that. Can we not talk about this anymore? Let's focus on getting you out."

Chapter 42

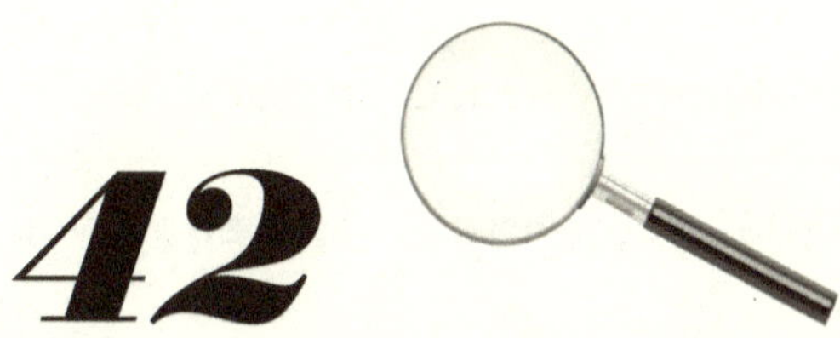

N*hyira* smiled when she entered the diner the following day. "I'm glad to see you back at work. How's your brother?"

"The old champ's going to be fine. He's recovering well."

"Are you ready to get back in the kitchen?"

"I'm sorry to have left the team so suddenly."

"There's nothing to apologize for. Family comes first. I think everyone was happy for the break. And the hype of Mr. Iwai's death has died down."

"Good to hear. We'll be opening the doors at 9AM. Our latest start to date, but I know today will go well."

"Can we sit for a bit? I have a few questions to ask."

Abacus stares at his watch, "Now?"

"It won't take long. It's better to ask you than anyone else," Nhyira taps her pencil.

"Ask me what?"

"Mayleigh told me you had a girlfriend 10 years ago. What happened with her?"

"I told her not to talk about it," Abacus snaps.

"She didn't bring it up. The conversation was about you two."

"Mayleigh and I?"

"Yeah, she said you were in a relationship and she was married at that time."

"That's the truth," he nods.

"What about now? Ever considered dating her?"

"She's one of my oldest friends and my boss. Whatever could've happened between us ended a long time ago."

"Are you sure?"

Abacus peers at her. "What is this really about?"

"Curiosity."

"I know that you're a curious woman, but this isn't any of your business."

"You're correct."

"Is that all?"

"What was her name? Where's she now?"

He stands up and towers over Nhyira. "You're a nice young lady, but at times I think your curiosity could get you into trouble. Things didn't work about between my ex and me. Her name is forbidden from my lips. I'm married to my work. That's not a chapter in my life that I want to relive."

"I didn't mean anything by it," she apologizes.

"Of course you didn't. You just want to know everyone's business. How about you handle your business and stay out of ours?"

"Where's this coming from?"

"I don't really get involved in my coworkers' life, but that thing you have going on with Jörn is ***pathetic***. You women always want to **jump** to the next man. No explanation. No caring about how we feel about you. Akio loves you; the entire town could see it. You're engaged to a nice man, but you don't love him. **THAT** is the business you should be handling; the matters of **your** heart," he snaps.

"SORRY BOSS," one of the sous chefs yells from the kitchen when the alarm goes off.

"I'm going to go see what they're up to in there before they burn this diner down. Think about what I said though."

As Abacus goes to do damage control, Nhyira stares out the window thinking about the next phase of her life. Was she truly going to marry Jörn?

She ignores her rampaging thoughts and commences her work day, placing the menus on the diner tables. Anything to distract her from the decision she avoided making.

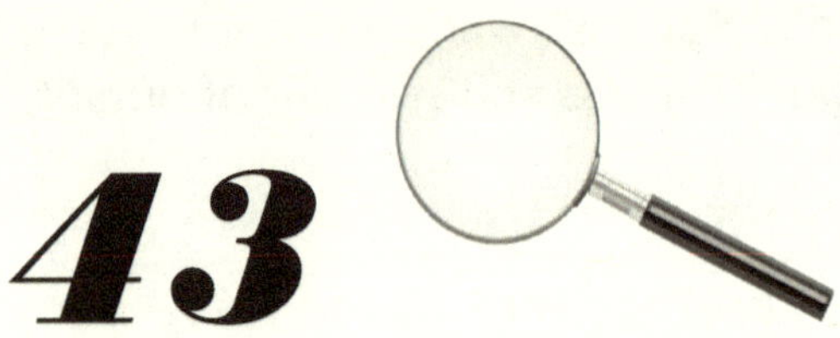

Chapter 43

H*er* shift couldn't end soon enough and Nhyira was happy to be home, talking to her fiancé.

"You seem distant," Jörn notes. "What's the matter?"

"Mayleigh's trial was pushed up and I'm not close to solving this case. I feel stuck," Nhyira replies, apprehensively.

"Why don't you leave the police to do their job? I think you've helped more than expected."

"She's my best friend and I don't want her to end up in prison."

"I just feel that you should leave it alone. It's been weeks, maybe you're not meant to solve this one."

"I don't understand what you're saying. I thought you admired the fact that I'm helping her."

"Can I ask you something?"

"What is it?"

"Is this how our life together will be; putting other people before us? It seems as if other people's lives matter more than our relationship. We used to talk every day. It'll be a miracle if I even hear from you two days in a week. There's no longer talk of **us** anymore. When we do speak, the calls revolve around you solving a case you don't have to."

Nhyira feels slighted. "I can't believe you'd say something like that."

"I'm being honest. Women want men to be attentive and caring... Yet the woman I love is more engrossed in the lives of others."

"You're flipping the script on me."

"Look Nhyira, I'm not going to pretend that we're good when we're not. Let's talk about us. Work towards planning our life together."

"I can't do this with you, Jörn."

"Do what?"

"Have this discussion. I think we should end it before either of us says something we'll regret."

"There you go again; shutting me down. You want honesty and because it's not what you want to hear you cut me off."

"If you can't understand how important the people I love are to me, then maybe we don't need to be together." Nhyira angrily hangs up the phone.

Chapter

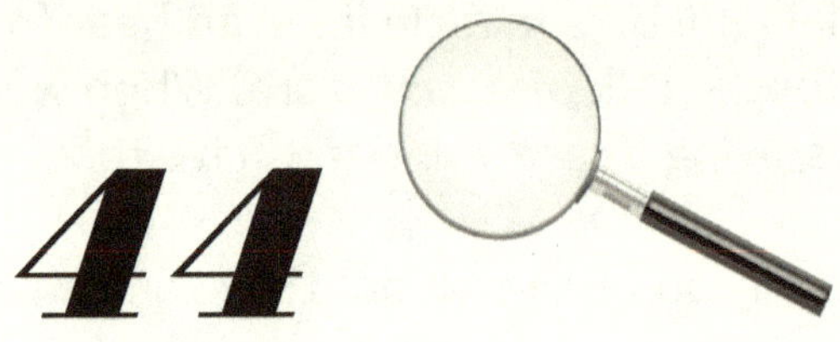

44

"...**And** God we pray that You help us to understand the Bible more. As we read Your word, give us clarity. I thank You Lord for my niece Nhyira. I pray that You protect her always. Help her to experience what true love and joy is..."

Nhyira stands in the foyer listening to her aunt and neighbor praying. She hadn't known when they started to pray, but she didn't like it.

What do they take this house for? This is not a chapel. I don't mind Aunty Poet living her life how she wants, but can she not include me? I don't believe in God. What did she mean by me experiencing true love and joy? I am happy. My life is good. I have done well without any **Higher Power,** *for almost 25 years of my life.*

“I hope they’re finished by the time I return,” she calls out to no one.

Chapter

45

W*eeks* passed since Nhyira visited the library. Walking through the aisles, she notices a library cart. On the top of the cart was a note attached.

To file in the archives tomorrow.

-Mrs. Denoble

Removing the note, Nhyira sees a book with pictures of local businesses. She flips through the book containing pictures of *Njapa's* businesses through the years.

Suddenly she sees **Mayleigh's Diner** in the **M Section**. The pictures contained visitors to the diner over the years.

Zooming in one of the photos, Nhyira notices a woman who looked like Mrs. Iwai, dated 12 years earlier.

Next to her were Mayleigh, Abacus, and other townspeople she didn't know.

Mrs. Iwai was in Njapa before? Does she know Mayleigh?

"I'm going out to run. Are you coming?" Nhyira asks Poet, a few hours later.

"Maybe tomorrow sweetie, I'm going to the jailhouse."

"You haven't been running in a few days."

"Don't worry, I'll start back soon."

"Be careful aunty."

Running through the large park allowed Nhyira to think about her life. As she ran, she looked down at the engagement ring on her finger. Marriage was a life changing decision. Saying "I Do" meant until *death do us part*.

Am I making the right decision with Jörn? Is he the man whose face I see when I think of my husband—

A woman's voice interrupts her thoughts.

Nhyira turns and sees Mrs. Iwai taking a sip of water from a bottle.

"Do you live near here?"

Nhyira points in the direction of the mansion. "I live in the mansion at the end of the park."

"I didn't know they had those in this quaint town."

"*Njapa* has many mansions."

"I've only been near the hotel," Ziema shrugs.

"Weird running into you, but I'm glad that I did. I have a question."

"I've heard about you and your curiosity," Ziema grumbles.

"It won't take long."

"Hurry, I want to get back to the hotel before night falls," she chimes.

"Have you ever been in *Njapa* before?"

"Why do you ask?"

"I was looking at some historical documents in the library and saw a picture."

"Is that supposed to ring a bell?"

"You were in the picture."

"You must be mistaken."

"I know what I saw."

"Ohhhh. My twin sister."

"Twin?"

"Yes, as in two of us," Ziema gestures.

"I didn't know that about you."

"My sister visited here frequently back in the days. She had a boyfriend who worked in town."

"Do you remember his name?"

"Not really. He was a basic man. Not important. After they broke up she never spoke about him."

"What's your sister's name?" Nhyira inquires.

Just then, a loud sound pierces the park.

"That's my alarm. I'm sorry Nhyira, I have to go. That car has been giving trouble since early this morning." Ziema takes off in haste.

There's something suspicious about her. All of a sudden her alarm goes off? Why didn't she want to tell me her sister's name? I **KNOW** *Mrs. Iwai is hiding something, I just don't know what it is.*

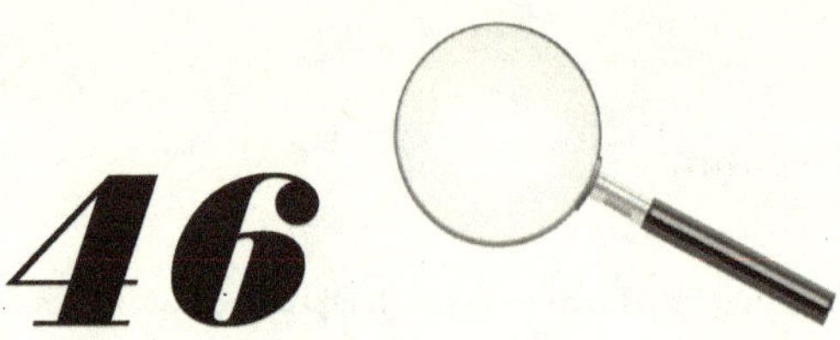

Chapter 46

N ***hyira*** clicks on her computer's search engine: *FindIt.Help.*

Ziema Iwai's sister

Moments later, a single picture shows up on the screen. Just as Ziema said; there were two of them.

The photo was dated 12 years prior as well.

"*Starr Islands' Photographer for the stars, Ziema,*" the caption read. No information was written about Ziema's sister.

Looks like Ziema was telling the truth. I need to find out from the townspeople if they'd seen her sister in Njapa before.

She snaps a picture of the photo on the screen.

"You haven't been here in over a year." Ms. Higüey says, opening the door later that evening. "Come in."

Nhyira enters the house.

"Would you like a beverage?"

Thinking back to her first encounter with her neighbor and her inhospitable manner, Nhyira smiles at the 180 she'd made. "Water will be fine."

Lively gives Nhyira a glass of ice and bottle of sparkling water.

"Thank you." Nhyira pours the bottle's content into the glass.

"What is it that you wanted to find out?"

Nhyira hands her the photograph. "Do you know these women?"

"Can't say that I do, who are they?"

"The food critic's wife and her twin."

"The man who died at the diner?"

"Yes." Nhyira hoped the photo would jog her neighbor's memory.

"Do you think there's a connection somewhere?"

"I don't know." Nhyira shrugs, mid gulp.

"I've been in this town for decades, but her face isn't familiar to me. Maybe you should ask Mayleigh, since she is in the photo."

"Good idea. Thank you for your assistance. How are you doing?"

"I don't think you've ever genuinely asked me that before," Lively replies.

"I'm sorry for not truly accepting your apology, Ms. Higüey. I appreciate that you're trying. You've been a great help to my aunt since she was released from prison."

"Poet's the one who has been helping me."

"You're helping one another."

"I never had a real friend. I am grateful for her."

"I'm sure she feels the same way. It's great that you could put aside your differences."

"I wish I could've been better help. I noticed you didn't include me in your book."

"You read it? I feel honored."

"You're an excellent writer, Nhyira."

"Thank you, I'll be going now."

"We should do this again, you know? Without the investigative formalities," Lively says.

"I'd like that," Nhyira replies, heading out the door.

Chapter

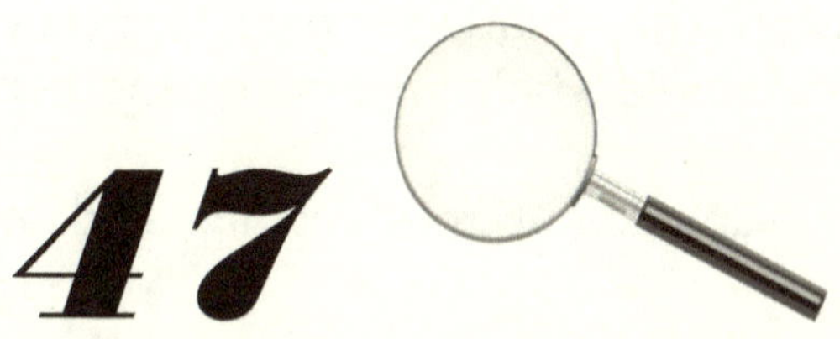

1 week later

"I didn't like how we ended our last conversation. You haven't been answering my calls so I flew out here," Jörn informs Nhyira, while they sat on the hood of his car. "I know that you're mad at me—"

"I'm not mad at you. I'm actually glad that you're here."

"You are?"

"I am," she nods.

"How is the investigation?"

"It hasn't changed much from the last time. I have tidbits here and there, but nothing concrete. How's work for you? When do you go to the palace?"

"This time next month. Did you start your second book?"

"I'll start it after Mayleigh's released from jail."

The conversation went on for several more minutes; drier than biscuits. It was their most awkward conversation to date; as if they were strangers on a blind date and not a couple who'd known one another all their lives.

"Have you been thinking about the wedding and moving with me to Voque?"

"Step right up," the man at the Star Ring Toss calls out.

"1 token please," Akio states, smiling. "I'm going to win you a teddy bear," he blushes at Nhyira.

"That—"

"—won't be necessary?" Akio finishes.

Nhyira laughs and playfully pushes his arm.

Akio winks at her and proceeds to play the game. "First laugh I ever got from you, I'll take it."

"This is for you." Akio hands her a stuffed white jaguar; Starr Islands' national animal. "You can name it Akio if you want."

"Keep your stuffed animal," Nhyira declines.

"I won it for you. Please take it."

"Will you leave me alone if I do?"

"I can't make that promise. In case you haven't noticed, I like you."

Jörn interrupts her flashback. "Nhyira, did you hear what I said?"

She jumps off the hood of the car; the epiphany hitting her like a ton of bricks.

Akio was the one she loved!

"Jörn, we have to talk..."

Chapter 48

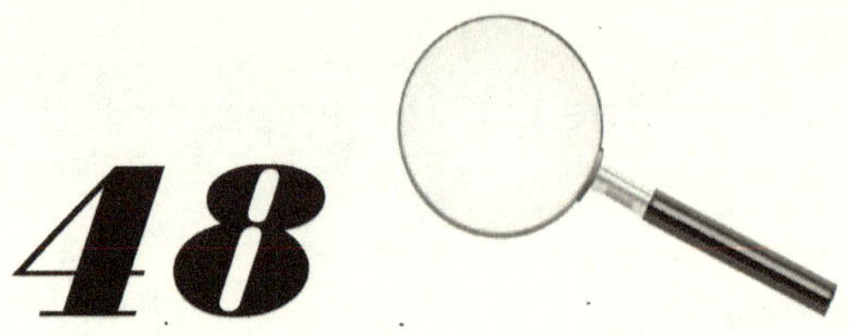

Jörn holds Nhyira's hands. "Speak to me my love."

Nhyira yanks her hands away.

"What did I say?"

"It's not you. It's me," Nhyira begins.

"Oh no, classic textbook *break up* line."

"You're a good man, but I haven't been myself since we started dating."

"What's the matter?" he asks.

"*This*. **Us.** Everything. I can't do it anymore. I care about you, but I don't love you. Not in the way you want."

"Love grows and I've loved you ever since we were children. I am willing to wait until you **catch up** to me."

"That's not what you should want. Yes, I believe a man should love a woman more, but ***catching up*** to your love? That sounds crazy. That's not how a healthy relationship works."

"We don't have a toxic relationship."

"The toxicity comes from both of us being in denial about what's happening."

"What are we in denial about?"

"The missing key in our relationship."

"Why are we going in circles? Just say what's on your heart."

"I thought long and hard about this. This is not an easy decision for me, but I can't do this anymore. It's not fair to you. You deserve better than what I'm giving you."

"You're breaking up with me?" Jörn exhales. "After all we've been through?"

"*Been through*? Although we've known one another since childhood, this relationship didn't start because of friendship, but familiarity. That's not what I want. And you shouldn't want that either."

"What is this *really* about?" he stresses.

"I don't love you and I don't want to marry you." She gives him the engagement ring. "I certainly don't want to leave *Njapa*. My life's here—"

"Can't say that I'm surprised, if I'm honest with myself, its Akio isn't it?"

"What does he have to do with anything?"

"I've been trying to ignore the obvious signs this entire time. Even though I hate to admit it, he loves you and I think you love him."

Nhyira sighs in recognition of her feelings being put on blast. "Are you mad?"

"Of course I am. However, marrying a woman who doesn't love me isn't right."

"You're a really good man Jörn and you'll find a woman who loves you back."

"Are you sure it's not you?"

"I'm sure," Nhyira says.

"Are you going to tell him how you feel?"

"Nothing's going to happen between Akio and me. He's not interested. He made that clear months ago."

"Whoever marries you will be very fortunate." He kisses her forehead.

At her front door, Jörn kisses her cheek. "I wish you nothing but the best. Bye Nhyira."

Closing the door behind her, Nhyira plops down on the floor and wails. What was she going to do? She broke up with a man who loved her and the man she loved wanted nothing to do with her.

Back to the single life; I'm done with all of this relationship stuff.

Chapter

49

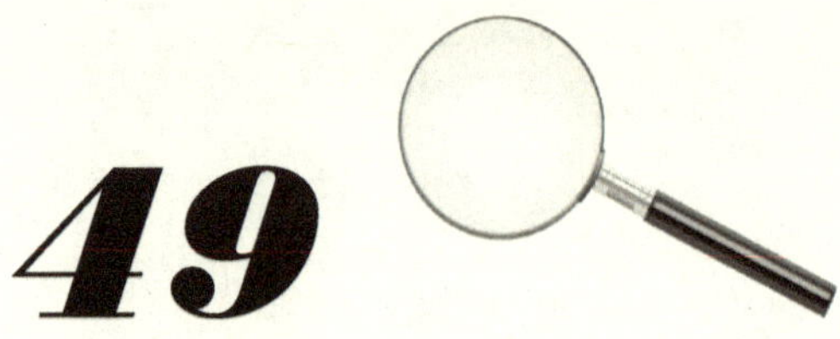

After her cryfest, Nhyira makes her way to the kitchen where she smelled her aunt's cooking.

Time to tell aunty that there won't be a wedding.

Instead of being greeted by her aunt, Nhyira sees pots of food on the stove and a note on the fridge.

Gone to the jailhouse with Lively. We'll be spending the night, praying for Mayleigh's release. Please put away the food on the stove.

P.S. You were invited to Abacus' birthday party at his apartment this afternoon. The official invitation is in the library near your computer.

~Aunty Poet

The gist of the invitation: It was Abacus' birthday and he invited the entire staff to his apartment to celebrate.

I guess I'm going to a party.

Finding an outfit for the party wasn't easy. As a casual woman, she didn't own anything fancy. Searching through her closet she made a note to go on a shopping spree before her 25th birthday.

She settled on a coral maxi dress; noting its simplicity and elegance. After inserting a pair of silver teardrop earrings in her ears, Nhyira scoops her hair into a tight bun.

I hope I'm not overdressed for the party.

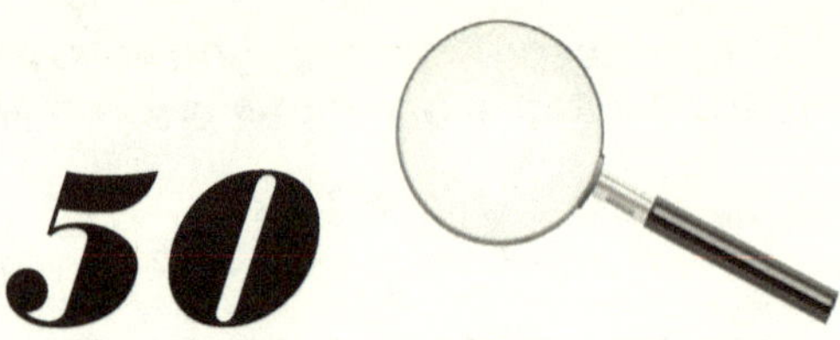

Chapter 50

"**Happy** *birthday to you, happy birthday to you, happy birthdayyyyyyy dear Abacus, happy Birthday to you,*" the guests sing in unison.

"Speech, speech," one of the younger sous chefs calls out.

Abacus smiles and raises his glass. "Thank you everyone for showing up. I know it was last minute, but I decided to celebrate my birthday this year with you. You are the kindest group of people I've ever met. Here's to many more celebrations in the future."

"CHEERS!" the group yells.

One of the waitress' hugs Nhyira. "You look beautiful girl."

"Thanks hun." Nhyira waves to the woman as she left the apartment.

"Looks like I have to clean up by myself. No worries," Abacus laughs out loud.

"No, no. It's your birthday. I'll help you clean," Nhyira volunteers.

"Don't you just hate it when people come to your house, eat, and then leave before the cleanup?" he replies.

"I wouldn't know," she shrugs. "I don't entertain."

"How are you Nhyira?" Abacus bends down to pick up a plastic cup from behind the couch.

"I'm good."

"Why didn't you invite Jörn? I thought I saw him earlier."

"We broke up."

Dropping the garbage bag from his hand, Abacus claps sarcastically. "That is the best news I've heard all day."

Nhyira chuckles lightly. "Wow. Thanks."

"No, really, you couldn't have made a better choice. He wasn't right for you."

"You have someone else in mind?"

"As a matter of fact, the entire town does."

"I don't like the idea of everyone betting on my love life."

"No bets," Abacus says.

"How does it feel to be one year older?"

"The same as last year," he shrugs.

"Any wishes?"

"My wish has already come true."

"Ohhhh. Do share. Do share."

"It's a secret," Abacus smiles.

"But if it already came true why can't you share?"

Abacus' phone rings. He runs to pick it up. "Hello. Thank you. I can't wait to see you either… "

Nhyira smiles at him.

"That was my sister," Abacus informs, moments later.

"I didn't know you have a sister. Does she live here in *Njapa*?"

"She travels for work."

"That's great. I want to do more traveling one day," Nhyira responds.

Nhyira looks at her watch. "Oh, it's getting late. I should probably head home."

"That's fine. You've helped enough. I appreciate it."

"I'll wash the dishes before I leave. It's your birthday after all." Nhyira shakes the bottle of dishwashing liquid. "Looks like you're out."

"I have more underneath the sink."

Opening the cupboard Nhyira felt dizzy. Underneath the sink were several bottles of **Brorfliete**.

Nhyira begins to tremble and stands up. When she turns around there was a silver object in front of her eyes. Behind the object was Abacus Boada.

Chapter

51

Holding the gun, Abacus leads Nhyira to a chair he'd obviously been preparing for this moment.

Why didn't I put this together before? It all makes sense.

"I've been waiting a long time to do this. And creating a fake birthday party was the only way I could've lured you to my apartment."

"It's not your birthday?" Nhyira fidgets with the rope tied around her hands.

"Yes it is. But, I usually don't have parties. However, given all that's been happening I needed a way to bring you here. I knew that you're clever so I thought long and hard for weeks how I'd go about getting rid of the woman who was sure to ruin my life. I even convinced Mayleigh to hire you for the restaurant; a way for me to keep tabs on your whereabouts."

"How could you?"

He laughs manically.

"I don't understand. Why? Why'd you kill Mr. Iwai?"

"SHUT UP!" Abacus slaps her across the face and ties a rope around her mouth. "I guess you're not as smart as the world thinks you are. ***Unscrambler?*** What a joke? You didn't solve this case. And pretty soon you won't be around to tell anyone. No one knows you're here."

Nhyira struggles to get the rope off her hands. The idea of death scared her. She'd been coasting on her intelligence for years, but nothing could keep her from being shot by this crazed mad man standing over her.

"You should have minded your own business. But **no**, you have to be the **Heroine of *Njapa***. Not this time." He throws lighter fluid around his apartment.

Nhyira screams, but it was muffled by the rope.

Is this how my life ends?

"Bye Nhyira. I hope you said your last words to your loved ones because you'll never see them again." Abacus throws a match on the fluid and slams the door.

God, if You exist, please send someone to help me...

The rope began to cut off the circulation in Nhyira's wrists and she fades.

Chapter

52

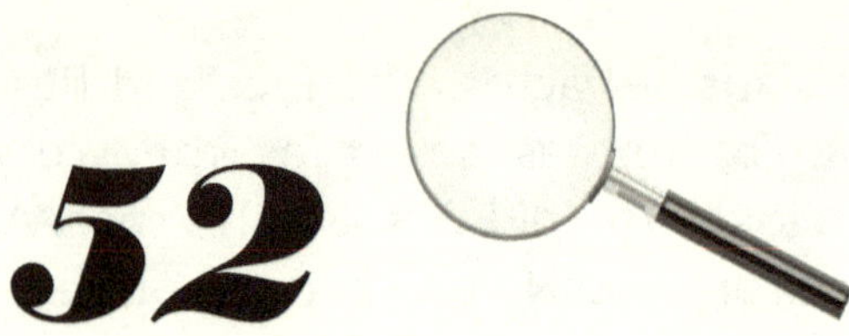

A*kio* bursts into the apartment and sees Nhyira tied up with smoke surrounding her. He pulls on the emergency sprinkler system, sending water raining down all over the apartment.

I hope back up would be here soon.

He unties Nhyira from her shackles and performs CPR.

"Come on Nhyira. Please don't die on me," he cries as he gives her air.

After trying for a few minutes, Nhyira begins to cough.

Akio takes her in his arms and hugs her. "Oh thank God," he laments.

Nhyira stares at Akio's face and smiles in confusion. "What are you doing here?" she asks, before fading again.

The next morning Akio sat by Nhyira's bedside, praying.

Looking around the room, Nhyira squints at the bright hospital lights. She places her hands on Akio's head. "Akio? Akio? What happened?" Nhyira inquires weakly.

"You're up. We thought we'd lost you."

"Where's my aunty?"

"I sent her home to get some rest," Akio replies. "She'll be back this afternoon."

"But what happened?" Nhyira grimaces in pain.

"We can talk about it later. Go back to sleep."

"I want to know what happened."

Akio relays the story to Nhyira.

> "We were gathered in the jailhouse for an all-night prayer vigil with Mayleigh. I asked your aunt about you. She told me that you'd received an invitation to a birthday party for Abacus at his apartment.
>
> I had an encounter with Mrs. Iwai and she informed me that she was in a relationship with Abacus that ended 10 years ago because she hooked up with her now deceased husband.

I put two and two together and came straight to the apartment. Everything made sense. *Jilted lover kills his ex's husband.* I'd been outside for two hours watching the building. I saw the diner workers leave. When I didn't see you with them, I thought maybe you decided not to go, so I put on my engine to drive back to the jailhouse. However, I saw Abacus run out of the building waving a gun in his hand. I immediately called for backup.

Then I saw smoke coming out of the building and ran upstairs..."

"Y-You came for me?" she exclaims feebly.

"I didn't know you were in the apartment."

"You came for me," she repeats.

Akio wipes the tears from her eyes. "Abacus confessed to murdering Mr. Iwai."

"I don't understand something. I spoke to Mrs. Iwai and she told me she had a twin sister who had an ex in *Njapa*."

"When I talked to Mrs. Iwai, she told me that she was an only child."

"But I found a photo of her online with another woman who looked exactly like her."

"Photography tricks."

"That makes sense. She is a professional photographer."

"She was brought in last night for questioning. Mayleigh's lawyer was able to dig up background information connecting Mrs. Iwai to Abacus; apparently from the picture at the library that you told him about. This isn't public knowledge, but she told the officers at the station that she'd met Abacus while on vacation in *Njapa*. They were in a long distance relationship for two years. But, the relationship went sour because she met Mr. Iwai and fell in love. They were married after one week. Before this year's chocolate festival she never returned to *Njapa*. She had nothing to do with her husband's death and she was released."

Two things crossed Nhyira's mind at that moment.

1. ***The man she loved rescued her.***

2. ***Her best friend was now acquitted of all charges.***

Chapter

53

Although Nhyira was still in the hospital, nothing could remove the smile on her face, knowing that Mayleigh was now a free woman. She remembered a quote from her parents, *"The truth always comes out, no matter how long it takes."*

The Echo Journal

A JILTED LOVER'S REVENGE

July 20, 2000

Two months after Mayleigh Antao was arrested for the murder of restaurateur and food critic, Cyprian Iwai, residents woke up to the surprise of their lives. Mrs. Antao has been acquitted of all murder charges and was released from jail last night.

After weeks of extensive investigation, police has arrested Executive Chef of Mayleigh's Diner, Abacus Boada. A story straight out of a tragedy novel, Abacus confessed to killing Cyprian Iwai on the night of the Chocolate Festival.

Ziema Iwai, Cyprian's wife and Abacus' former lover has denied any involvement in the murder and has been granted all of her husband's wealth and investments.

According to his confession, on the night of the murder, Abacus saw Cyprian for the first time since his breakup with Ziema some 10 years ago and became enraged. He ran into his car, grabbed a bottle of Brorfliete that he uses to wash his vehicle, and doused Mayleigh's prized mixing spoon with the disinfectant.

Mayleigh innocently used said spoon to mix the batter of Plumberry Pancakes that ultimately led to the critic's fatal bite.

Abacus stated that he didn't intend on killing the critic, but wanted to hurt him for the decade of pain he experienced when he lost the woman he loved.

Thanks to the assistance and detailed investigation of Njapa's Crime Solver, Nhyira Enosis, Mayleigh is now a free woman. We could all use a friend like Nhyira.

BY: LEGEND GOLD

8

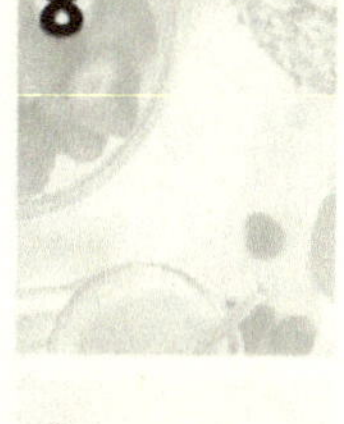

9

10

Open House!
*Please contact D. Sellers at *88-01-20-4420 for more details.*

THE ECHO JOURNAL | 1

TEJ - SI

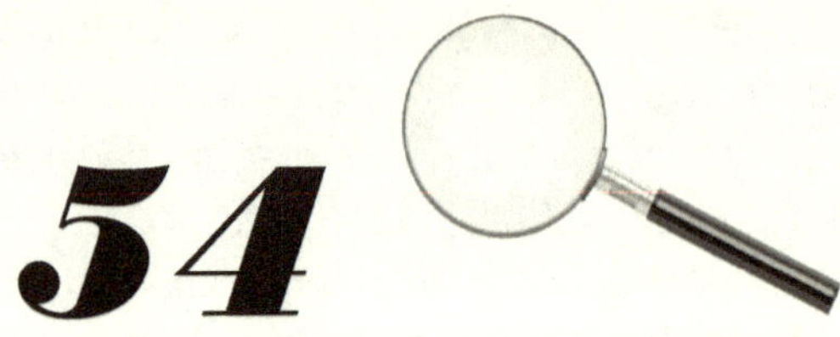

Chapter 54

4 Months Later

Today marked a special day in history; one that surpassed any other day. The day Nhyira was baptized.

After the ordeal with Abacus and weeks of seeking out the God who saved her, Nhyira gave her heart to Jesus.

Akio chose to stay away from *Njapa* and Nhyira so that he wouldn't sway her decision. However, he couldn't miss her baptism day.

Poet smiles at her niece. "I am proud of you Nhyira. This is the most important choice that anyone could make. How does it feel to be a Child of God?"

"I know that I am a writer, but there aren't enough words to describe how thankful I am to be alive." She looks around at her family and loved ones gathered in her kitchen: Poet, Mayleigh, Lively, and Akio. "Thank you for speaking to me and praying for me. But, I am grateful that you allowed me to make this decision on my own. You didn't force me to choose." Looking up towards heaven Nhyira cries. "Thank You God for showing me Your love."

Poet hugs her niece. "So what's next?" She winks in Akio's direction.

Nhyira blushes and announces, "That's up to Jesus... "

OTHER BOOKS

Written By

THEASTARR VALERIE

MYSTERY

Want to learn all about how Nhyira became *Njapa's* bestselling crime solving author? Be sure to get your copy of book 1 in the Nhyira Files Mystery Series: *Murder in Zaire Valley*; available on Amazon. Here's a sample of the story.

Murder In Zaire Valley

Flipping through the radio stations, Nhyira Enosis puts her **Epitome X Series 1** into sports mode, excited at the chance to test drive her new car. She was minutes away from her potential dream house: a 40-year-old mansion in *Njapa, Zaire Valley,* Celgagoas.

A native of *Grape Fjord,* Mt. Thafivin, she was known as **The** Spelling Bee Champ. Nhyira had a natural ability to unscramble any word from the dictionary.

And no one could deny her fascination for unsolved mysteries. When she read the ad for the abandoned house up for auction, she knew that it had to be hers.

With her inheritance in her purse she mashed the gas pedal. If she missed the auction, someone else would bid on the house. That was a setback she couldn't afford.

Mr. Sellers had the perfect house for Nhyira. As the top Real Estate Agent in *Zaire Valley,* he knew how to match the perfect house with its perfect owner. This particular house however, remained unsold for decades. No one in the country was interested in procuring a house formerly owned by a man whose wife murdered him in cold blood.

The mystery of the old **Veisiejai House** remained since 1958. It was a part of *Njapa's* history that none of its residents dared to speak about. Only a handful of citizens knew what *really* happened on that fateful night...

End of Sample.

Upcoming Book in this Series

Laceration

ROMANCE

Worth The Wait Series

Book 1: *The Road That Led To Love*

I never met him, but I'm completely in love with him. When I was 8 years old I saw him for the first time on TV. I watched every show and movie he acted in and swooned. He is THE definition of FINATION. I had to make up a word to describe him. Yes, I know wishful thinking. As if I would EVER meet him. As if he would EVER like me...

"Earth to Tahira," Kaiora sings.

"We are supposed to be studying," Tahira replies.
Kaiora Marzocco had been Tahira's firecracker best friend for the past two years. Her mouth was known to get her in trouble at times; she held nothing back.

"I know that, but you zoned out. Daydreaming about that boy again?" she jeers.

"Who?" Tahira asks.

"The one you've liked since you were 8 years old."

"No. I was pondering on our exam tomorrow."

"Good. You need to learn now that it will never happen. Our life isn't a movie. Boys like that don't court or marry regular girls like us," Kaiora scolded, while popping a gum in her mouth.

Tahira stands up and declares, "I am not a regular girl. I am the daughter of a King."

"So am I, but the Bible speaks about idolatry."

"I haven't idolized anyone."

"Either way, let's stick with reality," Kaiora states nonchalantly.

"Besides, he isn't a believer."

Tahira frowns. "He does believe in Jesus."

"Believing in Jesus and serving HIM are two different things."

"Can we stop with the sermons? I know God's word," Tahira conveys, becoming agitated.

Pointing to the textbooks Kaiora ends the conversation. "Back to our studies."

Tahira begins to twiddle her fingers, zoning Kaiora out as she thinks.

Why is it so impossible for me to marry Tavario Mikos? He could become a Christian, like really serving Jesus. SIGH!! Who am I kidding? As Kaiora said, this isn't the movies…

End of Sample.

Book 2: *Not So Happily Ever After*

Tahira observes herself in the mirror, while gently rubbing her stomach. The daily battle of infertility plagued her mind. Ever since their wedding a little over a year ago, they tried to conceive.

Both her parents and in-laws constantly asked about their grandchild. No one truly understood the pressure of being barren at 29. Of course she didn't share her feelings with her husband. Guilt and shame overwhelmed her.

PCOS was not an expected diagnosis. Prior to their nuptials, they went to the doctor for a thorough medical checkup. The results came back in their favor. Nothing should have stopped them from conceiving.

Their anniversary came and went like any other day. They opted to celebrate in April instead of January. Originally, they'd planned to go on an all-inclusive vacation, but then Tahira got sick and spent a week in the hospital. She avoided going to the doctor for a few days until Tavario insisted.

Weekly date nights were an important part of their marriage. After dodging the conversation, Tahira finally agreed to a date night to make up for their failed vacation.

When they got in the car, she peers out the window in silence.

Tavario touches her hand. "*Dolcezza*, why are you silent?"

"I don't want to go anywhere," Tahira snaps.

"Why are you pushing me away?"

"You speak of loving me with your words, but I can see it in your eyes how much I disgust you."

"I love you. But, you've put up a resistance against me, ever since you returned from the doctor."

"Everywhere we go I see the look on your face around children. Like you wish you were a father."

"We have time. I'm not sure why you're worried," he responds, keeping his eyes on the road.

"The doctor said I can't have any children because of my condition."

"We're going to get a second opinion. I pray that you stop speaking negative. You don't have PCOS. Don't declare that."

"You're not a medical professional."

Tavario parks the car in front of the restaurant, turns to his wife and responds, "And medical professionals aren't God. Misdiagnosis happens all the time."

End of Sample.

Love In Lucca Series

Book 1: *Becoming a Royal Princess*

"There is no fear in love; but perfect love casteth out fear..."
1 John 4:18

Vaia throws herself on the bed; a million questions dancing around her head. Who was this man? Could she trust him?

She looked in the mirror, deciding on whether to change. Her suitcase was filled with unused garments.

I don't have time for one night flings. What do I know about this man? Am I really going on a fake date with him? This is unlike me.

Five minutes later, against her better judgment, Vaia makes her way to the 12th floor. What was the worst that could happen on a ship with numerous cameras and workers? If she felt uncomfortable, she had two choices: run or scream.

End of Sample.

Follow **Empress Royále Publishing** on Facebook and Instagram for information about upcoming books from Theastarr Valerie.

www.ingramcontent.com/pod-product-compliance
Lightning Source LLC
LaVergne TN
LVHW090941080826
845145LV00003B/839

* 9 7 8 1 7 3 3 8 2 9 3 3 5 *